Red Diamond Rustlers

Law was a rare commodity on the vast cattle ranges and a man had to fight if he meant to hold on to what he owned. A rancher dispensed his own justice when he caught those who stole his livestock, but Titus Sawyer lost more than cattle when rustlers raided his Red Diamond spread. Men were killed, too, slaughtered in a dreadful ambush, so when he summoned his nephew Frank to track down the killers, his desire to punish the culprits was deeper than justice; it was revenge.

Red Diamond Rustlers

Will DuRey

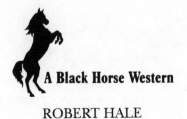

A Black Horse Western

ROBERT HALE

© Will DuRey 2019
First published in Great Britain 2019

ISBN 978-0-7198-2899-7

The Crowood Press
The Stable Block
Crowood Lane
Ramsbury
Marlborough
Wiltshire SN8 2HR

www.bhwesterns.com

Robert Hale is an imprint
of The Crowood Press

The right of Will DuRey to be identified as
author of this work has been asserted by him
in accordance with the Copyright, Designs and
Patents Act 1988

Typeset by
Derek Doyle & Associates, Shaw Heath
Printed and bound in Great Britain by
4Bind Ltd, Stevenage, SG1 2XT

ONE

Water washing at the very top of the animals' legs put an end to their headlong gallop. Beaver Creek was high this year and the men crossing it were wary of those little eddies and undercurrents that developed when it was in such a condition. Anxious though they were to continue the chase, they were no less determined to avoid any mishap that would force them to abandon it. Gently, therefore, with the understanding of men who had no desire to be left behind because of their own incaution, they coaxed the horses to the far bank. Once ashore they wasted barely a moment before using their spurs to urge the best effort from the animals once again. The rustlers' route was clear to every man there, the ground ahead scuffed and scarred by the hoofs of fast moving cattle.

Lon Foster, ramrod of the Red Diamond, looked at the western sky and pointed at the sun. 'We'll catch them before it drops behind those hills,' he predicted. It was a sentiment shared by every man who rode with him; they could travel faster than men hustling a herd of cattle. Local ranches had lost a lot of cattle in recent weeks, and now there was an opportunity to catch those responsible.

When Pete Hartley, a rider for the Wheel, had brought word that four unknown men were running 150 head of Red Diamond beef south, Lon Foster had acted swiftly and instinctively. One man had been despatched to the ranch to report the news to Mr Sawyer while another five hands had been assembled to ride with him in pursuit of the stolen stock. Pete Hartley, too, had joined that party. Although the stolen cattle belonged to Titus Sawyer, Pete knew that his own boss, Willard Draysmith, would want to be represented when the rustlers were captured. Plenty of Wheel beef had been stolen in recent weeks.

Twenty minutes beyond the river they saw the first sign of those they meant to catch. Lon signalled a halt and every man's eyes scanned the rangeland ahead while the horses, regaining their breath, wheezed and snorted below them. They were closing in on their prey. A dust cloud, faint, dissipating, marked the location of the small, stolen herd and it gave impetus to the cowboys' pursuit. The rustlers had turned to the west.

'Making for the hills,' observed Jim Davis.

The Comstocks weren't high but they offered the outlaws a possible sanctuary from discovery. Valleys and draws abounded, some of which provided secret locations while others wound through the range of hills and led to the state line. Every man harboured the same thought. Lon Foster spoke it aloud. 'Best if we catch them before they get there.'

As though reacting to a sudden thought, Lon drew his six-gun and checked the loads. The implication that a fight would shortly be upon them caused others in the group to follow his example. When all were satisfied, they put their animals to a ground-eating run once more.

The rolling meadowland allowed the group to maintain their pace, although its character of dips and rises prevented any sighting of their quarry other than the dust cloud that they could see in the sky from time to time. They pulled rein along a saddleback ridge from which they were separated from the first swells of the Comstocks by a flat half-mile of grassland. The absence of rustlers and cattle was a disappointment.

'Where did they go?' asked Pete Hartley, but he received no immediate answer.

The sweating horses were weary but restless, shaking their heads, stamping their feet and turning circles in full awareness that there would be no rest until their riders dismounted. It was Dirk Grayson, a rider on one of the turning horses who alerted the rest of the group to the dust that was rising to the north of their position.

'There,' he said, pointing out the place that

seemed to be a trail around the foot of the nearest hill. Every man guessed that it probably led into a valley through which the cattle could be driven.

'Let's go,' said Lon Foster and he spurred his horse forward.

Within minutes they'd ridden down the escarpment, crossed the plain and followed the contour of the land that took them into a tight fold of the hills. Here, their pace was reduced and they were forced to ride in single file. After travelling a quarter of a mile, the trail widened and a kind of grove was formed with a handful of trees dotted along the lower hillside slopes. A movement to his left caused Lon to raise his hand, the command to halt to those in his wake. Two horses had been tethered to a tree. They were unsaddled but a basic rope harness had been fashioned for each. One end was attached to the bridle and the other to a large, loose branch, which lay on the ground behind the rear legs. Their plight was immediately clear to Lon; the rustlers had discovered the pursuit and used the horses to raise a false dust trail in order to lure their hunters away from the cattle. At that moment, stones tumbled down the hillside and the awful truth occurred to the Red Diamond ramrod.

'It's a trap,' he yelled.

Those were the last words he ever uttered. Guns roared their deadly message and bullets ripped into every man who'd ridden into that fold between the hills. Some tried to find shelter and some tried to escape from that killing place but soon, without any chance to protect themselves or retaliate, the ground was littered with the bloodied bodies of men and horses. The onslaught was over in less than a minute and those who had staged the ambush quit that narrow valley without a backward glance.

An hour after the deadly ambush, Titus Sawyer came upon the scene of carnage. Those who rode with him were shocked by the slaughter of their friends. Holstered pistols and rifles still secured in saddle boots told the tale of the ambush. The ranch hands had been lured into the enclosed pass and killed mercilessly. This had been cold-blooded murder and it cried out for revenge.

Unexpectedly, they found a survivor. Linc Bywater and his pal Tom Turnbull had remained at the Red Diamond after finding work there during the previous spring roundup. Young men who'd come west to make their fortune, one now dead and the other unlikely to survive a journey back to the bunkhouse.

'Linc's lost a lot of blood, boss,' Zig Braun told Titus Sawyer when the rancher knelt beside the shot cowboy.

'Do what you can for him.'

'His needs are beyond my skills, Mr Sawyer.'

The rancher's wrinkled, weatherworn face hid any emotion. He'd met troubles head-on all his life and he was too old to change his ways now. 'Get him to Braceville while we take the bodies back to the ranch,' he said. 'I'll send a man ahead to let the doctor know you're on the way.'

'I'm not sure how we'll get him there. Can't put him on a horse.'

'Can't leave him here. Rig up some kind of stretcher. If he's strong enough, he'll survive.' Both men studied the white face in front of them and neither would have risked a dollar for a hundred that Linc Bywater would be alive when he reached Braceville.

In the gloom of the evening, Titus Sawyer watched as his men toiled at the task of tying bodies across horses. Some of the animals were loaded double because three of their kind had been killed in the ambush. He didn't know the identities of the men who were stealing cattle but in silence he made them a promise. 'If it's war you want, then it's war you'll get.'

The wheel fixed over the ranch-yard gate had come west attached to the Conestoga wagon that had brought Willard Draysmith's parents and their young family west forty-five years earlier. It had become the family's symbol, their brand, a repre-sentation of which was burned into the hide of all their livestock. It was recognized beyond the reaches of the local county and Willard Draysmith, now head of the family, was acknowledged as one of the most powerful men in the state. This evening, his equally prominent neighbour Titus Sawyer passed slowly beneath it, trailing a second horse that carried a blanket wrapped body.

Alerted to the arrival of a visitor, Willard left his house and waited for the horseman to reach its wide front porch. Drawn by the bundle across the back of the second horse, a couple of curious ranch-hands followed the new arrival to the hitching rail outside the house.

'It's Pete Hartley,' Titus told Willard, then threw the lead rein to one of the nearby men.

'What happened?'

'Killed by rustlers over in the Comstocks.' Titus Sawyer's face rarely showed pleasure but this night it was grooved with grim lines that announced to Willard Draysmith that there was more to the story. 'Six of my men are gone, too,' Titus added.

'Step down,' Willard told his visitor, 'and come into the house.'

Older than his host by almost two decades, Titus Sawyer had never ceased to be the hard-riding cowman who had first brought a scrawny bunch of longhorns to this territory, and although the intro- duction of a Hereford strain had improved the quality of his stock, his own rough-and-ready atti- tude to life had never altered. Seldom was he seen wearing clothes that were not working apparel, and alterations to his home were undertaken only out of necessity; its furnishings were of the most basic kind. So it was usually with a degree of awkwardness that he entered the grand rooms of the Wheel ranch house. Even though Willard retained a firm grip on the functions of the ranch, he did so mainly from behind the desk in his study. His clothes were always dust free and his shirts laundry fresh. Titus attributed the elegance of life at the Wheel to the influence of Willard's two sisters and the wife whose home this had been before her untimely death. A multitude of lamps were situated in every room making them as light at night as they were during the day. The furniture was polished to a bright shine and the seats of the long settees were invitingly plump but too clean, he considered, for the britches of a man like himself. When he sat he always chose one of the hard chairs at the table.

This night, however, the smart surroundings failed to impact on Titus Sawyer's purpose. Not even the cut glass tumbler or the fine Kentucky bourbon that it contained distracted him as he recounted what he knew of the raid and its upshot.

'Something must be done,' he concluded. 'Five of my men ambushed and killed, and I don't suppose the young'un'll pull through either.'

'What does Fred Hayes mean to do about it?'

Willard's referral to the sheriff of Braceville brought nothing more than a shrug from Titus. 'Haven't spoken to him. What would be the point? We both know he's not going to forsake the town to chase rustlers he has no hope of catching. If he organised a posse they would only be exercising their horses in a gallop to the river and back.'

'You've got another plan fixed in your mind?' asked Willard.

'Not really. Hoped you might have a suggestion but tonight I guess I just wanted to know that we would work together to catch these men.'

'Of course we will, of course. Pete Hartley was a good man and I've lost cattle, too.'

Silence settled between them for a few moments. As much as Titus wanted to hatch some plan that would give him revenge on the rustlers, the anger he harboured over the murder of his men prevented the formation of any clear thoughts. Willard Draysmith, however, had not seen the carnage in the Comstock Hills. Consequently, he was less excited by a desire for vengeance. Indeed, he considered the death of Pete Hartley as he would any loss of property from the ranch: an affront to his authority. It was an event that earned a line in his journal and due contemplation of the cost to the smooth running of the Wheel. It was the associated loss of stock and income that whirred to the forefront of his mind. For a moment, his thoughts slipped back to his last visit to the Cattlemen's Association in the state capital, and a conversation he had had in the plush clubroom.

'Perhaps we need to bring in outside help like they did in Wyoming,' he said.

Titus lifted his head so that his eyes met those of the younger man. 'Regulators,' he said. It wasn't a proposition that sat easily with Titus. In the past he'd done his own fighting and saw no reason to veer from that principle in this instance. He wanted to get to grips with those who had killed his men and stolen his cattle. Besides, the hired men who had gone to Wyoming had had limited success and their antics had been frowned upon by the state authorities. 'They were different circumstances,' he told Willard.

'Cattle were being rustled,' the younger man stated in support of his suggestion.

'Homesteaders taking a handful here and there to boost their own small herds. The ranchers knew the identity of most of the people who were taking their stock and where to find them. Most of them were harmless people trying to get by.'

'They were still stealing,' insisted Willard Drayfield.

'I'm not defending them,' said Titus, 'just pointing out that our enemy is neither known to us nor harmless. Do we want to bring in a small army of men without a clear idea of when or where they'll meet the rustlers?'

The prospect of indefinite payments and provisions for a large group of men dampened Willard's enthusiasm for recruiting regulators. He would need to calculate the cost of lost revenue and compare it with the expense of that solution before pressing ahead with the idea. 'Perhaps the rustlers won't trouble us again,' he said. 'Reckon they might stay away from this county. After killing our men they'll know we'll show no mercy if we catch them.'

'You're wrong,' insisted Titus. 'The noose we'll hang them with for murder is the same one we'd have used for stealing our cattle. Having risked the rope for profit once they're sure to do it again. We just need to know when.'

'How do we discover that?'

'We need someone to undertake an investigation.'

'Fred Hayes?'

Titus shook his head. 'No. It has to be someone free to roam and I think I know the very person.'

TWO

They were still a quarter of a mile from the place where the rest of the crew were working the cattle when Zig Braun drew his companion's attention to the lone rider on the brow of the hill. 'Recognize him, Mustang?' he asked.

'No, but he's showing an uncommon interest in the herd.'

It was true: the man was almost standing in the stirrups, his body tilted forward, studying the cattle on the plain below. He could have been counting men or counting cattle but it was clear to Zig that the man had a clear purpose for being there. Little more than two weeks had passed since the massacre in the Comstocks and Red Diamond men were still twitchy around strangers. Every one was suspected of being a rustler.

'He can't have seen us,' Zig said, 'so let's circle round behind him and find out his business.'

They swerved away from their course, riding hard

around a knoll then climbing, unseen, up the low hill on which the watcher had been stationed. They approached from the rear, dividing before they reached him, Zig to the left and Mustang Moore to the right. Both men had unsheathed their rifles and held them in meaningful fashion.

'Sit easy, mister,' Zig said when they were within hailing distance.

If the man was startled by their sudden appearance, he was able to hide it, but he was clearly curious about their open hostility. Still, his hands remained on the saddle horn while he waited for them to come closer.

'Something troubling you?' he asked.

In response, Zig ignored the question and posed his own. 'What's your business here?'

'Do I need to have some business for being here? I understood this was open range.'

'Yeah, but those beeves are Red Diamond stock and our responsibility.'

'It's good you take your responsibility seriously but I just stopped to rest my horse.'

'Seemed to us that you were studying them closely, counting them, perhaps.'

'Why would I do that?'

'To know how many men were needed to run them across the border.'

'I'm not a rustler.'

'Perhaps we'll let Mr Sawyer decide that.'

The man shrugged and, sandwiched between the

two Red Diamond riders, allowed himself to be escorted to Titus Sawyer's rugged little ranch house.

When he saw the riders approaching, Titus Sawyer squinted his eyes and used a hand to blot out the sun's glare. Zig Braun's black-tailed roan was known to him, as was the skittish little animal that Mustang Moore always claimed was the best horse on the ranch, but his attention was fixed on the big sorrel in the middle. Its build and stride pattern were in direct contrast to the quick light footwork of the other two. Not only did the animal not belong to his remuda, it had never been schooled to work cattle. The rider, he figured, must be a Braceville townsman, but the closer he got the more sure he was that he was mistaken.

'Caught him spying on our herd up by the high trees pasture,' Zig told his boss when the horses came to a halt just inside the ranch yard.

'Spying!'

'Denied it, of course. Told us he'd stopped to rest his horse.'

Titus directed a question at the man in the middle on whom his eyes had been fixed since his arrival. 'Didn't you tell them your name?'

'They didn't ask.'

'Ornery as your father,' said Titus.

'That's funny,' the man said, 'he told me that you were the ornery one in the family.'

A Titus Sawyer grin was a rare event. 'Guess

you're Rufe's boy, but your face is already proof of that.' To Zig and Mustang he said, 'You can put the guns away. This is my nephew, Frank. He might be hanging around the place for a few days.'

'Sorry for not speaking up,' Frank told them, 'but I got here quicker with your guidance.'

'Get back out to the herd,' Titus told his workmen, then led Frank into the ranch house.

When the formalities were over, and a meal had been dished up and eaten, Frank and his uncle sat on the long west-facing bench seat at the side of the house.

'You got here real quick, Frank. I thought it might be another week before you showed up.'

'I was at home when the telegraph operator brought your message. Pa said you wouldn't have hollered for help if it wasn't important. After I'd cleared up a couple of tasks I was free to come east. My partner's capable of handling the other cases we have on our books. I caught a train to Silver City then hired the horse for the remainder of the trip.'

Titus wasn't sure he liked the expression 'hollered for help', but he kept his thoughts inside his head. According to the letters he received from his brother, Frank had a well-established investigation bureau in San Francisco, and if he was as able as Rufe professed then he might have the necessary skill to discover the identities of the robbers who were currently a plague on the territory. On reflection, he supposed, 'hollering for help' was exactly what he'd done but, irrespective of the truth of that statement, his nephew had undertaken a long journey to reach the Red Diamond and deserved his patience for that alone.

'In his letters, your pa says you've done some work for Wells Fargo.'

'They employ me from time to time, use me to investigate robberies and track down those responsible.'

'I guess what I need from you is something similar.'

'I figured that from the way Zig and Mustang behaved. Rustlers?'

Titus nodded. 'That's right. Stock losses aren't uncommon, of course; a cow taken here and there is usually the work of hungry drifters, but now and then somebody with more ambition takes a more sizeable bunch. Sometimes we catch them and sometimes we don't.'

'This time it's different?' asked Frank.

Titus told his nephew that the widespread raids were occurring with greater daring and regularity. 'Willard Draysmith at the Wheel has lost a lot of stock, too,' he informed his nephew. 'We'd combine forces if we knew where and when the rustlers intended to strike next.'

'You think they will come back?'

'Willard has doubts. After the last raid he thinks they'll be reluctant to risk returning to this territory.'

'Why, what happened?'

Details of the massacre in the Comstocks were given.

'We want the men responsible, Frank, but we're not going to capture them until we know who they are and when they are likely to strike again.'

'Are there no lawmen in the vicinity?'

'Fred Hayes is the sheriff in Braceville. There's not much he can do. We're pretty sure the cattle are being driven beyond the Comstocks then across the big river, which is the limit of Fred's jurisdiction. We need somebody who's prepared to pick up the trail on the other bank, nose around and bring back the names of those responsible for stealing our cattle. My men are good and loyal workers but their skill is working cattle. Someone with different abilities is required. Do you think you can help?'

In such circumstances, Frank wasn't the sort of man to give false hope so he merely told his uncle that he was prepared to undertake the task. 'I'd like to talk to anyone with information about the raids,' he said. 'Those who know the places where cattle were stolen or who might have caught a glimpse of the rustlers. A map would be helpful, too,' he added, 'to give me an idea of the layout of this territory.'

'My maps are in my head,' Titus told him, 'but tomorrow I'll take you to the Wheel. You need to meet Willard Draysmith and he has a drawer full of maps. Tonight you can talk with Zig Braun and the boys but I don't think they'll be able to add anything to what I've told you. No one caught sight of the rustlers until the last raid.'

'And all those men were slaughtered.'

Titus raised his eyebrows, giving his face an expression of astonishment. 'That ain't quite true. Young Linc Bywater's proved to be tougher than anyone expected. He's still in the care of the doctor but it looks like he's going to pull through.'

'Can I talk to him?'

'Guess so, but that'll mean a trip into Braceville.'

Titus's prophecy that his crew would have nothing to add to what he'd already told Frank proved to be true, but next morning as he rode side by side with his uncle towards the Wheel, he did so in the knowledge that Zig Braun and the other riders of the Red Diamond were eager for him to locate the rustlers. Good men had been killed in that narrow Comstock gorge and their former comrades were eager to throw lead at those who had carried out that deed.

On the map that Willard Draysmith produced it was clear to see that the water of Beaver Creek ran through both his and Titus Sawyer's ranches. The Wheel abutted the northern boundary of the Red Diamond spread and the Comstock Hills were a natural western boundary for both. The stolen cattle had been taken from grazing grounds close to the hills, so it was an easy assumption that they were hidden within the folds or had been driven right through and across the river beyond, which was the state border.

'There are countless tracks through those hills,' Willard told Frank, 'and you might search a year before finding any cattle hidden among them, but my guess is that they've kept them running all the way to the big river. They'll think themselves safe if they get across the border.'

Titus voiced his agreement but added a cautionary rejoinder. 'Their problem would come when they tried to get the critters across. It's not a friendly river. You need to know its mood before putting your stock at risk.'

'That's the point, though, Titus. It's not their stock. They don't care if they lose a few animals.'

Frank pointed at the map, indicating the unmarked land across the river. 'What do we know about this territory?' he asked.

'According to the government it's open range but Thomas Finniston claims it's part of his Spur empire. Hoping that grazing cattle there will give him the right to it without laying out hard cash.'

'Thomas Finniston is one of the richest men in the country with herds of many thousands,' Titus informed his nephew. That information was unnecessary, however; the name of Thomas Finniston was known even in distant San Francisco.

'Unlikely then that he is rustling your cattle.'

'Absolutely.'

'I wonder if he, too, is suffering losses.'

To his nephew, Titus Sawyer had described Braceville as a humble town that was no bigger than it needed to be. When they reached it, Frank had no cause for argument. It consisted of little more than two streets, one for commerce and the other for dwellings. Frank noted the premises of a barber, a baker and a saddler on one side of Grand Street, while a saloon, grain merchant and emporium were prominent traders on the other side. Titus touched his hat to several people as they rode the length of the street. One of those wore a star on his vest but Titus didn't stop to introduce his nephew. The presence of Titus in Braceville was clearly a matter of interest to several townsmen who watched as he passed by. When he failed to stop at the emporium or Al Tasker's Diamond Queen they were satisfied that they knew his destination.

Doctor Jones lived in a low, all-timber building that also served as his surgery. His raised voice carried to them from within even as the Sawyers dismounted and hitched their animals to an outside rail.

'Hope that's not our boy he's bellowing at,' Titus said, but there was humour in his tone. 'The doctor's a good man but he has a quick, volcanic temper. He's likely to yell poor Linc into the death that the bullets failed to achieve.'

Shirtsleeves rolled up to his biceps revealed the fact that Theo Jones was a powerful man. His large head twisted in Titus Sawyer's direction when the door opened and the fiery expression on his face eased somewhat when he identified the new arrival. He pushed a hand through his thick hair, which was beginning to turn grey above the ears.

'This one,' he pointed a hand at a pale, young man, 'thinks he'll be some use to you out at the Red Diamond.' It seemed probable that if the young man lifted his hands from the table upon which they were firmly set, he would fall to the floor. 'Tell him,' the doctor said fiercely, 'that he's no good to you in the condition in which you now see him, and that if he insists upon riding he'll be dead before he gets out of town.'

'I want to be back at the ranch,' insisted the patient.

'Linc, the doctor is giving you good advice. Stay here until you're fit. A few more days will make all the difference.'

'Days!' exploded Theo Jones. 'Yesterday, Harry Benbow was here with his rod to measure him for a wooden box. It'll be weeks before he's capable of working again.'

'Well,' Titus said to Linc Bywater, his gruff voice resting over the doctor's abrasive rant like soothing oil on a sore, 'I reckon you need to stay here a while longer, but I promise we'll get you back to the ranch as soon as the doctor says you're fit enough to travel.'

'I can't just sit here, Mr Sawyer, I can't.'

'Sitting here is as good as sitting anywhere else,' interrupted Doctor Jones. 'Better in fact,' he added. 'Out at the Red Diamond you'll be sitting all alone while the rest of the crew are chasing cows. Here, you have the pleasure of my company. You've been looked after well enough, haven't you?'

If Linc Bywater had an answer that he was prepared to give voice to, it never came. At that moment the door opened and a girl carrying a cloth-covered tray came into the room.

'And here's Lulu with a meal for you. Looked after you for two weeks like a proper nurse and you just want to quit on her without a word of thanks.'

Lulu had large, dark eyes that, had they been lit by the merest glint of happiness, should have been an asset to the life of any young woman. They were, however, dull, and as there was no fullness to her cheeks, they gave her face a gaunt expression. This was added to by a long, tight-lipped mouth. Her clothes were not of the best style. Indeed, the short heavy jacket she was wearing could have been made for a large man but it had the effect of diverting attention away from the thin dress she wore underneath. It was too short to comply with the acceptable standards of the day, barely reaching her knees, and it had a red frilled hem that added a gaudy brightness to the black material.

Now, in response to the doctor's words, her dark eyes widened and glanced towards young Linc Bywater. Although it was only momentary, it was a look noticed by everyone in the room. Instantly, she put the tray on the table and uncovered the bowl of soup that sat upon it.

'Al Tasker has been sending soup from the Diamond Queen every day,' Theo Jones explained. 'Lulu seems to have been lumbered with the job of bringing it for my patient.'

'It hasn't been any trouble,' Lulu said defensively. 'Al just sends whoever is available.'

'Sure,' said the doctor who knew from comments in the Diamond Queen that she had volunteered to bring the food and had not only sat with Linc long after he'd had his fill from the bowl but also through the nights when he'd lain in troubled sleep.

'He wants to go back to the Red Diamond,' Theo said. 'What do you think about that?'

'He can't be strong enough. He's eaten nothing but a few spoonfuls of soup each day.'

'There,' Theo said to Linc. 'Your nurse agrees with me. Why don't you sit down and from tomorrow she'll start bringing meat stew that will fill your belly and put colour in your face. When your cheeks are red you can go back to the ranch.'

Linc made one more effort to persuade the doctor and his employer that he should be allowed to return to the ranch. 'I want to do something,' he said. 'I need to do something to brush away the images in my mind.' Even as he spoke, the strength left his legs and he sank onto a chair.

'Maybe you *can* help,' said Frank Sawyer.

'This is my nephew, Frank,' Titus announced to everyone in the room.

Linc looked at the younger Sawyer with interest, wondering what help he could be to the newcomer.

'Eat your food, Linc,' Frank said, 'then we'll talk.'

Titus told Lulu that he would pay for the meals that were being supplied by the Diamond Queen but she dismissed his offer.

'There's always spare food,' she said, 'and the kind act is good for Mr Tasker's reputation.'

'In that case put an extra plate on the tray for me,' said Theo Jones. The wide-eyed stare she turned on him expressed her belief that there was a limit to Al Tasker's benevolence. 'I'll pay for it,' he added.

When she'd gone, Frank took the seat she'd occupied while feeding Linc Bywater. 'My uncle wants to find the men who staged the ambush that you were caught in,' he said. 'At the moment we have little information to go on. What do you remember about that day?'

For a moment it seemed that Linc had expended every ounce of energy. His eyes were heavy but his desire to help overcame his need for sleep. He spoke quietly.

'Lon Foster found me and Jim Davis in the big meadow along Beaver Creek. He told us that Pete Hartley had come across some men driving our cattle west towards the hills. We gave chase but they must have had a lookout watching for pursuit. When we followed them into a narrow valley we realized too late that it was a trap. The cattle weren't there, just gunmen on the slopes who were able to pick us off before we could reach our guns.' He paused a moment, breathing heavily. Those gathered at his side were unsure if it was due to tiredness or the remembrance of the slaughter. 'I guess the rest of their crew must have taken the cattle to the south of that hill while we were being lured to the north.'

'What about the men who attacked you?' Frank asked. 'Can you remember anything about them, anything specific about anyone?'

'I was shot in the first fusillade,' he said. 'I didn't have time to see much.'

'Is there anything at all you can tell us?'

'It's not much,' he said, 'but I seem to recall a man standing up when the firing began. He was wearing a long buckskin jacket and he had a neat, pointed beard.'

'Was he fair or dark?'

'Dark. I'm sure he was dark haired.'

Frank Sawyer nodded when he realized that Linc had no more information to impart.

'I told you it wasn't much,' Linc said.

'It's more than we had. It's a starting point.'

Frank's eyes settled immediately on Lulu when he and Titus pushed through the batwings that gave them entrance to the Diamond Queen. She looked their way professionally – more customers to hustle, more silver to tease out of their pockets – but when she recognized them, the smile that had begun to stretch her freshly painted lips slipped away and she remained at the far end of the long bar. The rouge that had been applied to her cheeks since leaving the doctor's house didn't escape Frank's notice, nor did the low cut of the dress that had mostly been hidden by the jacket she'd worn earlier. Although her eyes remained dark, unlit by any spark of joy, he detected a pugnacious, determined attitude to her demeanour.

Frank acknowledged her with a brief nod but his uncle was talking in a low voice, demanding his attention.

'This is Fred Hayes,' he said, looking in the mirror at the man who had followed them into the saloon. 'He's the sheriff here in Braceville. Whatever excuse he has for coming to speak to us his only real reason is to find out who you are.'

Fred Hayes cut an imposing figure. Apart from Frank, he was the tallest man in the room, three inches higher than Titus Sawyer, and he was broad-shouldered and free of unnecessary girth. A walnut-handled Colt sat snugly in an old holster on his right hip and the star that was fixed to his plain blue shirt shone prominently. 'I've been expecting a visit from you,' he said to the rancher.

'Why would I do that?'

'You had men killed by rustlers. Seems to me that

that is a matter for the law.'

'Nothing you could have done about it, Fred,' Titus told him. 'Those men are buried now and their killers, I reckon, are across the big river. Don't seem likely they'll come back.'

'That's a different line to the conversation you had with Willard Draysmith. He told me you're seeking vengeance.'

'I've had time to think on it,' said Titus.

'Well, that's good.' Fred Hayes studied the younger man who was part of the group, his eyes settling on the crafted gun-belt around his waist, 'because I thought for a moment you'd taken up employing a different type of hired hand.'

Titus bristled. 'I don't need anyone to do my fighting; I've always done my own and I'm too old to change that now.'

'But you are here to fight,' Fred Hayes accused Frank.

'My name is Frank Sawyer. I'm visiting my uncle for a few days.'

'OK,' said Sheriff Hayes, 'but let me be clear, Titus, I don't want gunplay in this town. If you identify the rustlers I expect you to tell me. I'll lock them up and the law will punish them.'

'Well, that's clear enough and it's what we all want,' said Frank. He picked up another glass from a tray on the bar, poured whiskey into it and pushed it in the sheriff's direction. 'A toast to the rout of all villains,' he said.

THREE

Henry 'Mustang' Moore rode west with Frank Sawyer next morning to guide him to the site of the massacre. The suitability of the narrow valley for staging an ambush was immediately obvious to Frank. The carcases of two horses ripped by scavengers and rotting in the heat, still lay where they had fallen. Mustang indicated the places where the bodies of men had been found but such detail had no real value. Only the overall picture stored in his mind had any significance, fixing, as it did, the shock and anger that the cowboys must have briefly known in that instant before the guns began firing, when they realized they had ridden into a trap.

Frank recalled Linc Bywater's hazy depiction of the fight and glanced up the hillside. The trees and bushes that grew there would have provided ideal cover until the victims were directly under the ambushers' guns. Dismounting, he climbed up the hillside and studied the scene from the viewpoint of the killers. He didn't expect to learn anything new, just adhering to the investigation routine he'd adopted over the years. Don't hurry; attention to detail usually paid dividends in the long run. He found some brass shells, but that wasn't unexpected. A lot of ammunition had been fired probably in less than a minute and the killers wouldn't have hung around to collect their spent cartridges. There was nothing exceptional about the couple he collected. They were Remington .44s and had probably been fired from the same gun. He put them in his pocket and slithered back down to the valley floor.

Mustang Moore, who had ridden a little way along the valley while Frank had been up the hillside, confirmed that the cattle hadn't been driven into this place.

'No sign of a herd in here,' he said. 'I reckon the rustlers raised dust by dragging bushes. It's an old trick but it works.'

'Let's get out of this valley,' Frank said. 'We'll ride south and see if we can pick up the trail.'

They found flattened grass leading into a fold in the hills that Mustang announced led all the way to the river.

'You should get back to the Red Diamond,' Frank said. 'I'll find my way to the river and cross it if that's where the trail leads.'

'They must have gone across,' Mustang reasoned. 'Even if they'd hidden the herd among the hills to evade pursuit they won't still be there. They would have moved them on at the earliest opportunity. They'd need to get them to an out-of-state railhead. Knowing the ranches are losing stock the dealers here aren't going to take branded beef without the owner being present.'

Frank agreed. Mustang Moore, he thought, had the world-weary appearance of a man who'd been pushing steers for a long time, but his mind was alert.

'If you want my advice,' Mustang said, but waited until Frank gave a nod for him to continue, 'I would forget about following any trail through these hills. Let's just get to the river and find where they crossed it. Following these valleys might have been the easiest route for driving cattle but at this time of year they couldn't have crossed the river this far south. It's a bad river, Frank. In summer, when it runs smooth and slow, you can cross it almost any-place, but right now, after the winter melt, it comes rushing down from the hills and all its channels and creeks get it twisting and spinning so that undercur-rents form. They can whip a critter off its feet in an instant. Once an animal gets pulled by that current it stands no chance of survival. I've seen cattle, ponies and men washed away so quickly that they've been lost from sight before the thought of recovery had any chance of forming in anyone's mind.'

'You've spent a lot of time in this country?'

'Most of my life. Plenty of it on the other side of

the river before Thomas Finniston or the Spur had ever been mentioned in this territory. Used to round up horses and sell them to the army. That's how I got the name Mustang.'

Frank had guessed that nickname had had some such derivation. 'So how far away from a suitable crossing point are we?'

'Could be twenty miles. Up to that point the banks along both sides are too high and steep for cattle. Soft, too. A herd of any size would soon churn the ground to mud, causing them to slide and slither then panic. No knowledgeable cowman would put them in a river at a point where he wasn't sure they could get out again.'

Frank accepted the other's logic. 'When I reach the river I'll head north,' he said.

'Why don't I stay with you?' Mustang said. 'Your uncle won't object. He wants those rustlers caught and told me to help you any way I can.'

Frank was accustomed to working alone but it took only an instant to recognize the asset of Mustang Moore's knowledge in this big and alien land. He turned his head to the north where dark clouds were forming. 'Rain coming,' he said, 'looks like we'll get wet.'

'Let's get away from this river before it becomes too heavy,' said Mustang. 'In a deluge, the banks are prone to mud slips.'

'I expect it takes more than a spring shower for that to happen.'

'You might be right but a French trapper once told me that a whole Mandan village slid into the river not far from here. Every man, woman and child swept away without trace. I've been wary of dwelling too long on these banks ever since. It's a bad river,' he insisted and Frank guessed that the older man wasn't prone to forging his opinion on false superstition.

Rain spattered now and then, forcing them to seek the protection of their oilskins but not severe enough to interrupt their journey. By the time they found the place where the cattle had crossed the river the rain had ceased and their coverings had been re-rolled and packed behind their saddles. The river had widened at this point to such an extent that, mid-stream, its shallowness had created an islet that stretched for more than a hundred yards. Trees and bushes, fresh with leaves and yellow flowers, flourished there.

'I would have chosen this spot, ' said Mustang. 'There are easy routes from here to both the Red Diamond range and the Wheel. The rustlers probably camped in the hills awaiting their opportunity to run off a herd of unguarded steers.'

Frank looked across the river to the flat grassland beyond. It was little more than a step higher than the riverbank, making it an easy crossing point for the cattle. 'Let's go,' he said, and his horse began to splash its way through the water.

They had been riding for almost thirty minutes before they came across the first sign of life. Frank had remarked on the absence of men and cattle on land that he'd been told was much prized as part of Thomas Finniston's empire. Mustang had told him that even the vast herds of the Spur outfit were isolated in the thousands of acres they claimed a right to. It was at that point that the sound of voices reached them from a hidden spot ahead. A few strides further and they reached the lip of a huge bowl-like delve in the land. At the bottom, a high-sided wagon had come to a stop and despite the urging of a young woman who was pulling at the head harness of the nearside leader, the horses were refusing to move.

An older woman, sitting on the driving board, was yelling, too but her words weren't directed at the animals, and it seemed more likely that the whip she was holding would be flicked at the four horsemen who were the object of her ire. One in particular, a thickset man, seemed to be the focus of her attention but he, in turn, was the most vociferous of her tormentors. His taunts were raising guffaws from two of his comrades who had reined their ponies to a halt at his side. The fourth member of the group was walking his horse slowly around the stationary vehicle, inspecting it with a critical eye.

Frank and Mustang put their heels to their mounts to begin the descent at the very moment that the trouble below escalated from words to violence. The older woman, with her patience exhausted or her sensitivities injured more severely by her tormentor's words, struck out at the man. Her whip cracked and in a moment the lash became wrapped around his shoulders and across his back. His yell was more an expression of surprise than pain because the leather waistcoat he wore saved him from serious injury, but his recovery was quick and his response as violent as her assault had been. Before she could withdraw the lash, the man had gripped it in his right hand and yanked it forcefully.

If the woman had released it she wouldn't have been pulled off the driving board but she knew that if her tormentor gained possession of the whip he wouldn't hesitate to use it on her. So she held on even as she hit the ground with a dreadful thud. The man was uttering threats, making it clear that she couldn't expect mercy from him. Mixed in with their laughter, the two who had remained at his side were shouting encouragement, voicing their opinion that she deserved the same treatment she'd dished out to him.

The younger girl, alarmed by the older woman's predicament, quit her place at the head of the horses and rushed to where she lay. She bent to one knee as though to aid her stricken companion, but she rose up again almost before her knee had touched the ground and as the man nudged his horse towards her she threw the handful of dirt and pebbles she had scooped up into its face. The horse gave a startled whinny, and shied away for a step or two. The young woman wasn't yet finished. She followed up the initial bold stroke by confronting the animal again. This time, accompanied with a powerful yell, she spooked it by flinging her arms wide and high. The horse reared so suddenly that the rider was unseated.

The whip had been pulled from the older woman's hand and the rider, too, had been forced to release his hold on it while struggling to his retain his seat on the rearing horse. Now it lay on the ground like a long black snake. The man cursed, his anger apparent to everyone, but now it was the younger woman who was about to bear the brunt of it. He scrambled to his feet, his eyes fixed firmly on the whip, his intention unmistakeable, but the younger woman, too, had recognized its value if her attackers were to be repelled. Simultaneously, they made their bids to be its possessor. The woman was agile, which gave her a slight advantage over the cumbersome cowboy. She moved swiftly and bent low as she advanced in order scoop up the whip while on the move. For a moment, the woman's speed of thought and action seemed to have earned her success. Her fingers began to close around the thick stock, but at the very last moment her aim was thwarted.

Although less nimble than the young woman, the man's long, purposeful stride, devoured the gap between himself and the whip and his arm reached out. The whip, however, was not his target. His open hand flattened against the woman's face and he pushed her backwards with such force that she stumbled and crashed onto her back on the ground. She cried out as the breath was driven from her body and her assailant grunted in triumph. Picking up the whip, he advanced towards her, flicking the long, corded leather to let her know he was no stranger to its use.

So intense had been his determination to gain the upper hand that the arrival of Frank Sawyer and Mustang Moore had gone unnoticed, but he became painfully aware of them when he raised his arm to subject the younger woman to the lash. Mustang jumped from the saddle, both booted feet hitting the man in the back, kicking him forward to land on his face in the dust. Mustang was upon him again before he could recover, turning him over and landing a stunning blow on his jaw. In other cir-cumstances, Mustang might not have fared so well against the bigger, younger man but the surprise of his attack had completely overwhelmed the other. The man was groggy and a smear of blood from a cut lip marked his chin. Mustang turned away from him, the welfare of the women now uppermost in his mind. They had gained their feet and were standing together beside their wagon. His tacit enquiry, which consisted of a long, questioning, unblinking gaze that held the younger woman's eyes, was answered with a brief affirmative head movement. The grim expression that had been on her face moments earlier was now replaced by one of stoic acceptance. If she had suffered injury or was experiencing pain she wasn't going to reveal the fact to anyone.

With Mustang's back presented to him, the man on the ground made a move towards the gun in his holster.

'I wouldn't do that,' said Frank Sawyer who had his own pistol pointed at the man. He, too, had been alarmed by the prospect of the whip being used against the women but Mustang had reached the scene ahead of him and he'd reined his horse to a halt a few yards from the scuffle. Now he was in a position from which he was able to cover all four men, although one of them was partially concealed by the four-horse wagon team. 'Don't any of you get any foolish ideas,' he announced.

The man who had fought with Mustang got slowly to his feet and picked up his hat.

'Now,' Frank said, 'get back on your horse and ride.'

'This is Spur country. We give the orders around here.'

'Not today and perhaps never again if Thomas Finniston ever learns of your treatment of women.'

'Come on, Jake,' one of the mounted pair to the left of Frank said. 'Let's go.'

Jake, the man on the ground, scowled. 'Make

sure our paths don't cross again,' he told Frank. 'It'll be different next time.'

Frank moved his gun to hurry the man into the saddle. 'Next time,' he said, 'I might shoot you.'

Three of the men put spurs to their horses and rode swiftly up the slope. The fourth man walked his horse slowly around the team from the far side of the wagon. He was younger than his companions and his expression less hostile. His hat was hanging on his back by means of a cord, revealing fair hair that was long and curled.

'The wagon won't get far until that rear wheel is fixed,' he told Frank, and then he, too, kicked at his horse's flanks and rode away.

The young man's diagnosis was accurate. The wheel had been weakened by a shattered spoke and it was clear that it was likely to collapse if it met with any obstruction. It took Frank and Mustang a couple of hours to complete a makeshift repair. Lacking proper equipment and tools they fashioned a stout tree limb to a size suitable for wedging between the hub and outer rim. When the work was completed they shared a meal the women had prepared, and learned their recent history.

'If the colonel had still been with us,' said Meg Rouse, the older woman, 'they wouldn't have dared to chase us the way they did. The colonel knew how to handle such roughnecks.'

The younger woman, who ventured only Alice for

a name, said, 'He would have stopped and told us to put on a performance for them.' There was such ambiguity in her tone and words that Frank was uncertain if she had admiration for the man or was implying that any response by the colonel would be governed by a weakness of character.

Bold blue lettering on the high yellow sides of the wagon had already informed Frank and Mustang the nature of the women's business. *Colonel Abraham Potter's Medicine Show*, it read, adorned with motifs of bottles, musical notes and high-kicking women.

'Where is the colonel?' asked Mustang.

'Dead,' said Alice. 'He was killed back in Winter Gulch.'

'Anything to do with those men who stopped you?'

'Don't suppose it had,' she said. 'They had other things on their mind.'

'I'm afraid that I was the one who panicked,' said Meg Rouse. 'If the colonel had still been with us he would have taken command of the situation. He had a wonderful understanding of people's character and could argue and dissuade the most volatile antagonist from his intent with a few well chosen words.'

Alice cast a withering look at her companion. 'He had less backbone than you,' she said.

Meg Rouse was rankled by the younger woman's words. 'Colonel Potter was a good man. He looked after you when you needed him.'

Alice flapped a hand in Meg's direction. 'I'm not saying I didn't like him,' she said. 'He had many good points, but heroism wasn't one of them and it doesn't pay to kid yourself that it was.'

'How come he got killed?' Frank wanted to know.

'Cards were a weakness. We'd reach a town, any town, and right away he'd be looking for the saloon where the best poker game was being held.'

'Did he win much?'

'Reckon so. We were never short of money even if we didn't sell much of his patent medicine or attract large crowds to our entertainment shows.'

'Killed at the tables?' Mustang asked. In his mind it had been easy to attribute a medicine showman with an ability to deal cards from the bottom of the deck.

'No,' said Meg Rouse, 'he was killed on the street and robbed. There wasn't a cent in his pockets when his body was found and we understand he'd won a lot of money that night.'

'What are your plans now?' asked Mustang.

'To get far away from Winter Gulch. It's an unfriendly town.'

Frank, being practical, said, 'If you mean to keep travelling in that wagon then you need to get to a town where the wheel can be fixed properly.'

'Braceville is nearest,' Mustang told them, 'but that's across the state line.'

Alice rose to her feet and flipped the dregs of her

coffee into the dust. 'Perhaps we'll just abandon the wagon if it won't go any further.'

'What would we do then?' asked the older woman. 'All we know is entertaining. Men will still come to watch you dance even if we don't have any of the Colonel's patent medicine to sell.'

Alice's look was as heavy with exasperation as it was with annoyance. 'We can't go on with the show,' she said, the tone indicative of the fact that she'd said those words on other occasions. 'Large towns have theatres now and even the small ones bring dancers and troupes into their saloons. This life is finished, Meg. We have to face up to that.' She stopped talking then, angry with herself for speaking openly in front of strangers.

'Then what will we do?' Meg's voice was almost a whimper.

'I reckon that anyone who can prepare food like this on an open fire should be filling the stomachs of hungry cowboys,' said Mustang in an attempt to raise the spirits of the women. 'Braceville could sure use a good eating establishment.'

'Speaking of Braceville,' Frank said, 'I think you need to hit the trail if you want to be there before nightfall.' To Mustang, he said, 'Perhaps you should go with them to lead the way through the hills.'

Mustang agreed. 'They'd be stranded if the wheel failed them at the river crossing.'

So Mustang and Frank parted company, Frank

making tracks for Winter Gulch where Mustang promised to join him after escorting Meg and Alice to Braceville.

FOUR

When he reached Winter Gulch, Frank Sawyer took a room in the Tumbleweeds Hotel. Inside, it was even less salubrious than the dry, paint-flaking exterior suggested, but he had no plans for an extended stay in the town so dropped his saddle-bags and bedroll on the floor, washed his hands and face in a bowl on the dresser then went in search of food. He ignored the hotel's dining room and chose, instead, a table in the Eating House whose clientele seemed to consist entirely of out of town cowboys. Frank wasn't troubled by that; he wasn't in Winter Gulch to socialize and there was a slim chance that from their conversation he might learn of any trouble the Spur was having with rustlers. In addition, he knew that working men wouldn't frequent the place if the meals weren't plentiful and nourishing.

From his table by a window, Frank had the chance to study the street before darkness fell. Its character was that of many towns that had sprung up across

47

the west in order to provide the sort of commercial and social centre necessary for an enterprise to thrive. Sometimes it was a military garrison, sometimes a railroad depot or even a gold strike. In this instance it was a section of the Spur empire. Almost every horse that arrived in that town bore the same mark burned into its hip that he'd seen on the horses of the four riders whose harassment of the medicine show wagon he'd interrupted. It was a circle with eight short lines evenly spaced around its outer edge, the representation of a rowel, the Spur brand.

Although there was plenty of noise in the Eating House it was restricted to the boisterousness of men who had reached the end of another hard-working day. Shouts were thrown across the room, jibes with no ill intent that were rebuffed with words of equal merit, silenced only when a platter was laid before them and food filled their mouths. Frank's presence evoked nothing more than brief glances and he was left alone to enjoy his meal in peace.

Whatever hopes his uncle had for the recovery of his stolen stock were not shared by Frank. Those cattle were gone and would never return to the range across the big river. As Frank saw it, his mission was to identify the thieves and prevent future raids on the Red Diamond stock. With only the sketchy description of one man to aid him he was faced with a formidable task. Unsurprisingly, his eavesdropping efforts in the Eating House proved difficult and totally unrewarding. The noise in the room made it impossible to concentrate on any single conversation and nothing he heard gave rise to the belief that the Spur was anything but a well-organized ranch. So, when he'd finished his meal, he decided to continue the loose investigation in one of the saloons. Rain had begun to fall, not heavily, but it had been repetitive throughout the day and the dirt streets were becoming slippery with mud.

For no other reason than that Meg Rouse had named the Northern Rose as the last place Colonel Potter had visited before his untimely death, Frank chose that drinking palace as his starting point. He found a place against the long counter that put him close to three cowpunchers, but he soon discovered that they had put aside all thoughts of ranching and were in town to enjoy the fun it had to offer. Two had plans to sit in on a nearby poker game while the other was on the lookout for a girl called Lily whose absence was causing him some anxiety. Frank moved further along the bar, deeper into the room where some store-suited men were discussing the merits of a railroad branch line that had been built to nearby Tomahawk Wells. One man, who Frank deduced was a storeowner in Winter Gulch, was so enamoured of it that he told his companions he was considering moving to the railhead town.

'Tomahawk Wells is bursting at the seams,' he claimed. 'New people are arriving every day. I'd be in constant need of replenishing my stock. Demand must surely exceed supply in such a boomtown. With the telegraph on hand to wire my suppliers and the railroad to transport them to my door I'd have goods delivered before my customers were aware they'd ordered them.' There was deep satisfaction in the grin he offered his friends. 'Yes, sir,' he added, 'the railroad is the quickest means of transporting goods, and also more reliable.'

'I've spent time in a boomtown, Jim,' one of his companions replied. 'All that noise and all those people. . . . You wouldn't like it.'

'I'd like their money well enough,' Jim said, and the entire group laughed.

Frank stepped away from the counter and cast his eyes around the room. There were numerous tables, all occupied, many with gamblers trying their luck with cards. He knew he was as likely to hear an unguarded word sitting as he was leaning against the bar so, when he spotted a vacant chair, he worked his way across the room to that table.

'OK if I sit in?' he asked.

'Sure,' someone said, 'if you mean to lose a lot of money.'

The remark brought the usual grins and laughter from the other men around the table and he took the seat.

'I'm Frank,' he said and nodded to each of the others as they introduced themselves. The grey, wiry-haired man on his right, the man who had first spoken, was Jonas Tapwood. A pleasant expression was fixed on his broad, weathered face even when he was bemoaning the cards he held. It soon became clear to Frank that the man's words were merely a form of guile to which the remaining players were well accustomed.

'Ignore him,' said the dapper man sitting opposite, eyebrows raised so as to cast mock reproach on the other. 'He grumbles every night but still wins more pots than the rest of us combined.' Horry Briar cut hair and pulled teeth in Winter Gulch.

The game proceeded in friendly fashion and while Frank gained a little knowledge about the principal townspeople he learned nothing that had any bearing on his purpose. Nothing was said that hinted at any kind of discord in the town.

'I've heard talk of the railroad reaching Tomahawk Wells,' he said when he became aware that Jonas Tapwood ran a freighting enterprise. 'I guess it must have had some effect on your business.'

'You guess right,' the man said, 'but not in the way you think. My wagons are constantly in demand to fetch goods from Tomahawk Wells. People too, who don't want to stay in that town. They pick a spot to build their homes then need someone to transport them, their belongings, timber for a house and furniture to fill it. All of that is additional to the work I already do for the people of this town and the Spur ranch.'

'Sounds like things are booming here in Winter Gulch, too.'

'They are for me,' Jonas said. 'In fact, if you're looking for work and can handle a team I'm looking to take on another driver.'

'Sure, I can handle a team,' Frank told him, 'but I'm not sure I'll be here long enough to take you up on the offer.'

'If you change your mind you'll find my premises at the south end of the street.'

At about that time, Frank saw a figure he recognized. Descending the stairs, his eyes scanning the room with the same expression of simmering wrath he'd worn when threatening Meg Rouse and Alice, was the man he knew as Jake. A girl was two steps behind, her hand on the banister as though its support was necessary. She had a trim figure and her fair hair was piled high on her head, although a stray strand hung over her left ear and touched her shoulder. She wore a black dress similar in style to those worn by other doves of the Northern Rose. When she raised her left hand to her face it drew attention to the smudge at the side of her mouth which might, at first, be mistaken for misplaced make-up but which closer inspection proved to be a smear of blood across a fresh bruise.

Not looking for trouble, Frank averted his eyes from the figures on the stairs, concentrated instead on the cards in his hand. He hoped to escape the notice of the man he'd encountered earlier in the day and was successful. A strident voice, however, got the attention of everyone in the room, the babble of conversation dying instantly as the menace it held was apparent to all.

The speaker was the cowboy who'd been standing close to Frank at the bar, the one in search of Lily. Now he'd found her and was angered by the injuries that showed on her face. In addition to the damage around her mouth, a bruise high on her right cheek had been covered with cream and dusted with powder but the swelling couldn't be disguised.

'Did you do that, Jake?' the cowboy wanted to know.

With a surly grunt, Jake scoffed at his interrogator. 'She wanted my money but didn't want to earn it.'

'Did you want his money, Lily?'

'Forget it, Buck,' she said.

Buck wasn't prepared to forget. He could see Lily's pain and Jake's smirk. He spoke to Lily but his eyes never left Jake's face. 'Did you go with him willingly?'

A chair scraped and another man moved, stepping forward, putting himself between the two men. He was a tall, young man whose fair hair curled onto his shoulder. It was the man who had given Frank advice about the fractured wagon wheel. 'Let's sit down,' he said to Buck. 'No need for this to blow up into something unnecessary.'

Buck shoved away the younger man's arm, too

angry to accede to the first overtures of peace. 'Your brother's a brute,' he announced. 'Thinks he's master of the town ever since he teamed up with Carter Ford.'

'If you don't like the way things are here then just draw your money, saddle up and move on,' Jake told him.

'You don't have any say in that matter,' Buck answered. 'Out at the Spur you're just a hired hand, like me.' His jaw worked as though he had more words to throw out, words that were related to working at the Spur, but instead he sighed deeply.

The younger man tried once more to separate the antagonists but Buck looked again at Lily's face and what he saw wouldn't allow his wrath to subside.

'Stay away from Lily,' he ordered Jake.

'Do you think you can make me?'

'I'm not afraid of you. You'll find I'm a different proposition to an old medicine show man with too much whiskey in his belly.'

'What do you mean by that?' Jake's utterance was almost a snarl.

'You know what I mean. Everybody knows what I mean. You wanted the dancing girl and he kept her hidden from you. He even outfoxed you at the poker table but he made the fatal mistake of turning his back on you.'

'You can't prove that was me,' snapped Jake.

'No, but I know your pockets were full of money the next day after losing heavily in here. Where could a ranch hand get all that money?'

The room was silent. An argument over a girl wasn't a rare occurrence in the Northern Rose but this one had suddenly taken a sinister twist. Jake's bullying manner had grown in recent weeks and months, to such an extent that his company was mostly avoided by all but a handful of men. Now, as they absorbed Buck's words, the citizens of Winter Gulch awaited Jake's reaction.

The big man was bereft of words but the glare that filled his eyes told of his hatred for his accuser. Even so, to those in the room, there seemed to be hesitancy in his response, yet his right hand had moved very close to the butt of his pistol. It was his brother, however, who, also sensing Jake's indecision, reacted first. He grasped Buck's elbow and spoke low in his ear.

'I know you're angry about Lily but you have no cause to accuse my brother of killing the medicine show man.'

Buck turned his head, looked the younger man in the eyes. 'You've gotta quit defending him, Lou. He's not worth it.' Then he wrenched his arm from the other's grip in order to give full attention once more to the scowling Jake.

Jake, however, had seen his opportunity. With Buck momentarily distracted by his brother's intervention his hand had clamped around the butt of his pistol and, using the other's exaggerated arm movement as an excuse, pulled it from its holster and fired. The bullet smashed into Buck's chest, toppling him backwards, sprawling him on the floor of the saloon.

Surprised and in pain, the shot cowboy still tried to defend himself. With his right hand he reached for the gun at his side but never got the chance to use it. Jake stepped forward and fired again and again, ensuring that his opponent was dead.

'He went for his gun,' he said, his voice loud enough for everyone in the room to hear. 'It was me or him. You all saw him push my brother aside so that he could pull iron.'

No voice was raised in confirmation or denial of his assertion. The rising smoke revealed the pale faces of those who had been closest to the shooting. The expression on Lou's face still registered the same level of surprise that had adorned it from the moment the first bullet had punctured Buck's chest. So close had he been to the victim that a gout of blood had sprayed his sleeve, its wetness soaking through to his arm. For the moment, he was unable to find any words that could either support or condemn his brother's deed.

Lily, who was standing by the bar, dropped her hand from her mouth and gazed at the body on the floor. 'I didn't ask him to interfere,' she said to nobody in particular.

The barman banged on the counter with an axe handle like an army sergeant trying to rouse a sleeping troop. 'You men get him out of here,' he said to those gathered around the nearest table, 'and let's have some music, Charlie.'

The pianist began to play and the first low conversations began again. Within a minute the noise in the Northern Rose had risen to the level that had existed before the confrontation. A man had died but his violent passing had caused barely a ripple of concern among the people of Winter Gulch.

'Where's the sheriff in all this?' asked Frank.

Jonas Tapwood spoke while he dealt out cards. 'Either sitting in his unlit office or drinking whiskey in Memphis Annie's bawdy house.'

'Shouldn't someone fetch him to investigate the shooting?'

'Wouldn't do any good. He's a Spur man. He's not going to lock up someone on the payroll no matter who he killed.'

'So the cowboy will be buried and that'll be the end of it?'

'That's the way it goes around here.'

'Is that what happened when the medicine show man was killed?'

'That's right,' said Horry Briar.

'And did it happen the way that cowboy alleged?' The women had kept Jake's earlier interest in Alice from him but he didn't blame them for that. Nobody spoke of their own history in the west.

'You're a stranger in this town, Frank. You don't want to get involved in events you'll be leaving behind in a day or two.'

Frank could have told them that he was already involved, that it had been necessary for him to rescue the dancing girl that Buck had spoken of from Jake's clutches out on the range towards the big river. Whatever initial motive Jake had had for waylaying the wagon, and Frank had no reason to doubt it had been with violent intent, there had been a murderous lust in his eyes when he'd advanced on Alice with the whip. Now, he'd assaulted one of the house girls and killed a cowboy and believed himself justified in doing so. Buck had accused him of shooting Colonel Potter in the back. If he weren't checked, he would kill again.

'But he can't be allowed to get away with murder.'

'There's no evidence against him,' said the barber.

'And no investigation to find any,' argued Frank. 'What happened here tonight was murder. No matter what he says, he shot that man without warning. And his brother might be guilty of conspiring with him. He had hold of the cowboy's arm, perhaps prevented him from reaching his gun.' Frank raised his eyes to the bar where Lou still stood. For a moment they gazed at each other.

Jonas Tapwood looked up from his cards. 'There's no evil in Lou,' he said. 'He's not like his brother.'

'Does he ride for the Spur, too?'

'Sure. Most people work for the Spur one way or another.'

58

'And the other man that Buck accused of the medicine show man's killing, him, too?'

'Carter Ford! No. I'm not sure what brought him to this neck of the woods but it wasn't to work another man's beef. Perhaps he's a gambler. They turn up every now and then.'

'Yet it was the old man who was the winner at the tables the night he was killed.'

'That's right, but Carter Ford wasn't here. He hasn't been in town for a few days.'

'But he and Jake are friends.'

'Yes, although they are a mismatched pair.'

'How do you mean?'

'You've seen Jake, rough, coarse and dusty, but Carter Ford is just the opposite: tall, elegant sort of man. Dresses well and keeps himself clean.'

'That's right,' interjected Horry Briar. 'He visits me almost daily. Very particular about the little beard he wears.'

'Beard?' queried Frank.

'A little pointed affair on the end of his chin. A goatee.'

FIVE

To Frank's surprise, the slaying of Buck caused barely a ripple of interest among the people of Winter Gulch. Almost before the body had been removed the interruption seemed to be forgotten and activities resumed within the Northern Rose. To the accompaniment of loud conversation and heavily pounded piano keys, whiskey was served and drunk, cards were dealt and gambled upon and the saloon girls tempted and teased those customers who seemed likely to part with their money. Lily, over whom blood had been spilt, had fixed her hair and was working the room as avidly as any of her fellow practitioners.

'Lily didn't instigate the fight,' Jonas Tapwood confided when he noticed Frank's eyes on her. 'Something about Jake had been sticking in Buck's craw for some time and I reckon tonight he needed to spit it out. Jake's never liked opposition to his views and recently he's become more violent against those who rile him.'

'Including the medicine show man who won money from him?'

'Perhaps,' said the other, 'but the old man prevented him from having his way with the pretty dancer he'd brought to town. If Jake was responsible then robbery might have been a cover-up for a killing he was always going to commit. Carter Ford keeps him under control when he's around but, like Buck said, he's a brute when left to make his own decisions.'

Frank looked across to the bar where the brothers Jake and Lou stood side by side. When Jake saw Frank his shoulders stiffened, memory reawakened, and it seemed for a moment as though he was preparing to barge through the throng to reach him, but Lou spoke some words in his brother's ear and the elder man relaxed slightly. Still, his hand settled on the butt of his pistol and he lifted it slightly to let Frank know that it would come easily out of its holster again, as though one killing hadn't been enough to satisfy his appetite. Frank kept his eyes fixed on him until he turned away to lift his glass from the counter. Jake was a bully whose outrages needed to be checked, but Frank was keen to wash his hands of him, that was business that needed to be cleared up by the people of Winter Gulch.

For the moment, Frank was more interested in knowing about the man called Carter Ford. Any man who sported a goatee warranted his attention. Of course, he didn't want to announce his inquisitiveness with direct questions but from comments and snatches of conversation around the poker table he learned that Ford's likeliest destination after leaving Winter Gulch was the railhead town of Tomahawk Wells. Ford, he was assured, had a habit of disappearing for a few days and no one had any cause to assume that this time it would be different; his absence from town would be of short duration. If Frank remained in Winter Gulch it seemed probable that he would eventually cross paths with Carter Ford.

Idleness, however, was not in Frank's nature and he figured that people would begin to wonder at his purpose if he remained in town too long. Also, he'd learned of the existence of stockyards at Tomahawk Wells where eastbound cattle were held before shipment. Stockyards meant cattle buyers and they might be able to provide information about Red Diamond or Wheel herds that had reached that town.

Next day, after vainly awaiting the return of Mustang Moore until the noon hour had passed, he saddled up and rode west. The stableman gave him directions to Tomahawk Wells and informed him that unless he asked a lot from his horse he wouldn't reach that town until darkness had fallen the following day. Frank had no reason to punish his mount but rode at a steady clip across the open range land. The first day was drawing to a close when he saw fire smoke rising from among a distant clump of trees. He guessed it was the night camp of a couple of Spur drovers so swung his horse in that direction. He approached openly, letting any watcher know that he was alone and unthreatening.

Indeed, he had been seen. Five men, more than he had expected, stood near the fire when he slowed his horse to a walk and reached within speaking distance. He'd expected to see some cattle nearby but there were only empty acres as far as the eye could see.

'Saw the smoke,' he said. 'Hoped there was enough coffee in your pot to wash half a day's dust from my throat.'

There was silence for a moment. If the attitude of the men wasn't downright hostile it certainly wasn't friendly. They could have been cattlemen – their clothes were grubby and their faces were dirty and unshaven like men who had been eating cattle-raised dust for several days – but suspicion showed on their faces as though he bore the stamp of a harbinger of ill-tidings. All of them had the stance of men awaiting a fight, their shoulders tight and hands close to guns.

The nearest man, tall and dark-haired shifted his feet, eased his posture and ran the flat of his right hand down the leg of his grimy denim pants. 'Step down,' he said. 'Coffee's all we have to offer. We might be moving on shortly. Johnny, get the man some coffee.'

'My name's Frank.'

The man touched his own chest. 'Burt,' he said. He pointed to each of the others as he spoke their names. 'Will, Johnny, Clay. And that one,' the last was a mixed-blood man with big, dark eyes, 'we call Totem, because he utters as may words as a pole in the ground.'

Frank grinned because it was expected of him. 'I'm heading for Tomahawk Wells.'

'We've just come from there,' said Johnny as he handed over a half-filled tin cup.

His words were heard with Burt's silent disapproval.

'I was hoping to reach there tomorrow,' Frank said. 'Will I make it?'

'On that horse you should be OK,' Burt told him. 'He looks powerful.'

Frank nodded an acceptance of the compliment and let his eyes wander to the bunch of horses that had been picketed beyond the fire. They were tired animals as much in need of a wash down as their owners. Frank guessed that they'd been schooled to work cattle. Closer inspection revealed the rowel representation on each animal's rump. These were Spur stock so it followed that the men were too. He thanked them for the coffee, mounted up and rode on.

For five miles he rode, looking back now and then for the hairs on his neck were standing on end and he thought that there might be a chance that one of that group had followed him. The land, however, was too flat for anyone to remain permanently hidden so he kicked on, eager to cover another five miles before darkness descended. He camped on a knoll that was crowned with three tall trees. Enough twigs had fallen and dried on the ground to provide ample kindling for a night fire, but before seeing to his own comfort he attended to the needs of his horse. He'd unsaddled and brushed it and was allowing it to drink water from a dish when the sound of a distant rider reached him. Frank finished tending to his horse and looked across the plain in order to pick out the galloping horseman.

Although visibility was decreasing by the moment, the onrushing night seemed to enhance the clarity of sound and Frank was able to estimate with some accuracy the location of his fellow traveller. When finally he saw him, a dark shape, upright in the saddle with a loose jacket billowing behind, it occurred to him that the rider's pace indicated a disregard for the surrounding gloom. A man accustomed to the trail, Frank deduced, or one with a mission to fulfil that was more important than the risk of a mishap. Again, Frank experienced an inexplicable trickle of uneasiness and couldn't shake off the belief that an association existed between the five men whose coffee he'd shared and the galloping horseman; that the continuation of their journey was dependent upon his arrival. A need to know grew large in Frank's mind and momentarily he considered throwing his saddle back on his horse and following in the rider's wake.

Almost before the decision was formed, however, he abandoned it. He had an investigation to conduct and, apart from a disquieted spirit, he had no logical reason to suppose that the men he'd run into earlier had anything to do with that. Besides, what reason could he offer for returning to their campsite if he was discovered, the chances of which were very high? They had chosen an open location that was difficult to approach unseen. No, he told himself, he would not be sidetracked from his purpose. In the morning he would proceed to Tomahawk Wells. He made his fire, drank his coffee and laid his head on his saddle, but he underwent a troubled sleep.

The Winter Gulch stableman's prediction that Frank wouldn't reach Tomahawk Wells before next day's sunset proved inaccurate. It was mid-afternoon when he reached that town, a fact which he attributed not only to the quality of his long-striding mount but also to the dawn start that had been prompted by his restless night.

The overheard conversation in the Northern Rose had informed him of the growth of Tomahawk Wells but the reality still took him by surprise. Until the coming of the railroad it had, like Winter Gulch, been nothing more than a small settlement. Now it teemed with people, and the construction of buildings couldn't keep pace with the influx; most of the newcomers were living under canvas on the meadow at the far side of the railroad tracks. The din of industry assailed Frank as he manoeuvred a route through the overspill of pedestrians from the inadequate boardwalks. The sounds of hammer and saw were holding their own against the rattle of wagons, the voices of people and the barks, neighs and lowing of assorted animals.

It was the unmistakeable sound of cattle in the immediate vicinity that grabbed Frank's interest. Leaving the main street, he cut through an alley that brought him to the trackside. To his left he could see the long building and built-up platform that constituted the town's station, but he ignored that place and followed the track in the other direction where an assembly of corrals were situated. Many of them were filled with steers that were milling around with nervous anticipation. Here and there, a beast would rear its head and bellow. Frank cast an eye over them as he rode towards a gate where two men lounged in conversation. Drawing to a halt he transferred from the saddle to the rails of the nearest pen and inspected the cattle within.

'Prime beef,' he observed. 'How many have you got there?'

'Two thousand, waiting to be shipped out,' one of the men told him. He wore bibbed dungarees, a rough grey wool shirt and tough leather gloves.

'All one herd?'

'Sure. We've handled bigger, of course. Got pens enough for five times that number.' There was a bit of pride in the man's tone; the railroad had brought an opportunity to his town that he'd never expected.

'You work here?' Frank asked.

'Yep. Can I help you?'

'Looking for a cattle buyer. Where will I find one?'

'Michigan Assessors have an office on the street,' he said, pointing back in the direction that Frank had left behind. 'Mr Taylforth is the man you want.'

Frank nodded his thanks for the information. Before climbing back onto his horse he threw another look at the beasts below him.

'Something wrong with those animals?' The speaker was the second man. He was a scrawny fellow, unfussy in his appearance and dressed for the range. His face might not have seen soap for a day or two and it had been longer than that since it had come close to a razor. His dark trousers were dusty and his blue placket shirt had lost a button and was stained with dropped food or drizzled beer. The length of the sleeves was adjusted by a pair of red armbands and a gun-belt was buckled around his waist.

'No. Nothing wrong with them,' Frank replied. 'They're mighty fine cattle. Whoever reared them knew his business.'

'So!' said the man, suspecting that Frank had more to say on the matter.

'So why burn off or tar over the brand?'

The bibbed man turned his gaze on the man in the placket shirt with an expression that implied he too had asked that question.

'What's it to you?' the other asked Frank, hostile, ready for a fight.

'Seems to me that a man ought to be proud of his work.' He pulled the reins and walked his horse up towards the main street.

Frank's first stop was the hotel, but there were no rooms available and the desk clerk told him that there wasn't a vacant bed anywhere in town. 'Swamped out with people,' he said. 'If you mean to stay in Tomahawk Wells you'll need to buy a tent and pitch up in the meadow alongside everyone else.'

Frank hadn't any plans beyond the next morning but it was looking now as though they wouldn't include a prolonged stay in this town. However, because most new arrivals had reached Tomahawk Wells via the railroad, he had more luck finding stabling for his horse. He put it into the care of a man with an awkward limp who promised it the best care for fifty cents a night.

The building that bore the legend *Michigan Assessors* above its door was little more than a ramshackle hut on a block that included an ironmongery, a doctor's office and a dressmaker. When Frank opened the door the two men within ceased their conversation. One was seated behind a desk and the other, a man wearing a badge in the lapel of his jacket, was leaning arms folded against a wall.

'I'm looking for a Mr Taylforth,' Frank explained.

'You've found him,' said the man in the swivel chair. 'What can I do for you?'

'I'm told you buy cattle.'

'That's right. You got some to sell?'

'No, but I'd be interested to know who sold you those cattle in the station yards.'

Taylforth looked at the sheriff before asking, 'Who are you?'

'My name's Frank Sawyer.'

'Sawyer! Related to Titus Sawyer across the river?'

'He's my uncle.'

'Well, Frank Sawyer, I suppose you've got a reason for asking such a question.'

'I do. My guess is they are stolen stock. Someone's smothered the original brands with a running iron, a square burn big enough to ruin anything underneath. But they've been careless. Red corners can be seen on some and arcs are noticeable on others. If it was possible to remove the over-burns I don't doubt that you'd find the marks of the Red Diamond and the Wheel on most of those critters.'

The sheriff pushed himself away from the wall. 'That's a serious allegation, mister.'

'Certainly is,' said Frank, 'and I'll only prove it by finding the man who brought them here.' Turning once more to Taylforth, he asked, 'What proof were you given that the cattle were his to sell?'

'None. I wasn't the one who bought them.'

'The man down at the yards told me to speak to you.'

'Joe Hart is overseer there. He directs most new business to Michigan Assessors. If he thought you had cattle to sell he would direct you to me, but I'm not the only buyer in this town.'

'Then who did buy them?'

'My guess would be Foster Adams. He and Carter Ford were drinking in Brannigan's saloon yesterday.'

'Carter Ford,' repeated Frank. 'Man with a goatee?' He touched his chin with his thumb and index finger and drew them down to a point. When the cattle buyer nodded an agreement, he continued. 'You've done business with him in the past?'

'No. Ever since the railroad arrived in Tomahawk Wells, Carter Ford has been bringing cattle of dubious provenance here, but this company has standards and I certainly wasn't going to risk its reputation by conducting deals that I believed were underhand if not downright crooked.'

'But you were happy to let him sell stolen steers to another buyer.'

Taylforth shrugged his shoulders. 'Not my concern and, other than my suspicions, I have no

71

evidence of wrongdoing. If another buyer wants to take the risk then that's his affair.'

Frank addressed the sheriff. 'What about the law, have you had no cause to interfere in the matter?'

'Mister, I've got one deputy, and this town is so full of strangers seeking our assistance from dawn to dusk and beyond that we haven't got time to go investigating problems that no one has complained about. The cattle yards are a source of much-needed income for this town and I don't intend to scare away herds with unfounded accusations.'

'Well, go down to those pens in the morning and check out those fresh burned marks for yourself. Look closely and you'll see the tell-tale marks of the Red Diamond underneath.'

'They'll be loading the cattle at dawn. The trucks will be heading for Chicago before I've had breakfast.'

Frank knew there was little point in arguing with the sheriff. The population explosion in what until recently had been a one-street town had probably come as a surprise to him as much as it had to everyone else. The difference hadn't been tempered for him by the prospect of greater profit but by more responsibility. No doubt he was running the town the best he was able. 'Where will I find Foster Adams?' he asked.

When he left the cattle-buyer's office he paused for a moment, glancing in both directions along the street from which daylight was receding rapidly. Many people were still abroad and to accommodate them the shopkeepers and businessmen were lighting up the coal tar lamps outside their premises. The town noises hadn't subsided, simply become more concentrated around the three beer palaces the town now boasted. Brannigan's saloon, where Frank had been assured he'd find Foster Adams, was three blocks down on the other side of the street. With that destination in mind, he stepped down from the boardwalk but was instantly aware of two men who stepped deeper into the shadows of the building opposite, trying to disguise the fact that they had had him under observation since he stepped outside.

One man was unknown to Frank but his wide-brimmed white hat scuttled his efforts to be unobtrusive. Like his companion, he was no more than average height and possessed the rolling gait of someone who spent more time in the saddle than on his feet. The other man Frank had met before. He'd seen him while running an eye over the cattle in the railroad pens. Despite turning away and hoping for the sanctuary of darkness, the features of the slovenly man in the blue placket shirt had been recognized by Frank.

Although it had been the men's furtive behaviour that had drawn his attention to their presence, Frank had no reason to assume they were following him. Indeed, any accusation of that sort would be laughed at because it was impossible not to cross paths over and over again in a town like this. In addition, confronting them would only draw attention to himself and that was something he wanted to avoid. He walked down the street and entered Brannigan's saloon.

From the description given by the sheriff, Foster Adams was easily identified but he was currently engaged in a poker game so Frank had to settle for a beer until an opportunity arose to speak to the cattle buyer. It was a long, low room and the far wall seemed to have been demolished to allow the premises to extend into the adjoining building. Even so, the place was packed full of people, smoke and noise. Frank shouldered his way through to the counter from where he could keep an eye on Foster Adams. He hadn't been there long when the man in the blue placket shirt and his friend in the white hat entered. With studied indifference to the presence of Frank Sawyer, they bought their drinks and lounged against the long bar.

It was almost an hour before Foster Adams quit his place at the table and worked his way to the far end of the counter, greeting people and exchanging comments as he went. Frank followed him, and spoke to him as he was taking a sip from a fresh glass of beer.

'Where's Carter Ford?' he asked.

'Why should I know?'

'You bought the cattle that are corralled in the

railroad pens and he brought them here.'

'So?'

'So you've done business with him in the past and no doubt you hope to do business with him in the future.'

'What's that got to do with you?'

'We have a shared interest in the cattle.'

'You're partners?'

'Not exactly. My uncle rears them and Carter Ford steals them.'

'Now look here,' protested Foster Adams, 'those cattle were delivered to me with a proper bill of sale.'

'Those cattle have had their brands burned off and any bill of sale that accompanied them is as false as any others you've been given by Carter Ford.'

'You can't prove that.'

'You want to show me the documents? How much did you pay for the cattle, Mr Adams, sixty or seventy cents on the dollar? Quite a wad of money to put in your own pocket.'

'How dare you accuse me of such a thing? The sheriff will hear about this.'

'The sheriff already knows. I spoke to him earlier. So your days of crooked dealing in this town are over. You tell me when you expect Carter Ford to return with another herd and perhaps you'll avoid being detained by the law.'

The cattle-buyer struggled to find words of

dispute but Frank cut his bluster short.

'I can get the sheriff to put a hold order on the transport of those cattle,' he said, 'and when the documents you hold are proved fraudulent then the animals will be confiscated and you'll have lost the money you paid Carter Ford. Just tell me when he means to bring in the next herd and you can be out of here tomorrow.'

'A month,' conceded Foster Adams. 'He said he'd have another herd here in a month.'

Frank turned to walk away and found the man in the blue placket shirt directly behind.

'Are you following me?' he asked.

'No.'

'Why are you interested in what I'm doing? You followed me to the office of Michigan Assessors and you followed me here. Now you're listening to my conversation.'

'You're crazy,' the man said, his tone surly.

Behind him stood the man in the white hat. His hand was close to the butt of his pistol as though awaiting some signal to draw and fire. Frank decided it was in his interest to act first. Grabbing the front of the blue shirt with both hands, he pulled the man forward to unbalance him then pushed with all his strength. The first man crashed into the man in the white hat and both tumbled onto the floor, knocking aside other drinkers and overturning a table. Above the angry shouts of those whose drinks, cards and money had been scattered,

Frank's voice sounded loud and clear.

'If you're involved with him,' he indicated Foster Adams, 'then you need to get out of town tomorrow, too.'

He took a pace forward and trod on the right hand of the white hat man, who was scrambling to get his gun out of its holster. Then he pushed his way through the crowd and out the door.

SIX

Without a room to return to, Frank went to the stable to collect his bedroll. Despite the rain that had fallen intermittently since reaching his uncle's ranch, there appeared to be no alternative to another night under the stars. For another dollar, however, the stableman with the limp offered him a night's accommodation in the loft above the horses. A bed of dry straw promised more comfort than the cold, damp ground and Frank gladly flipped a coin to the ageing horse-minder.

Due to the restlessness he'd endured the previous night, sleep came quickly and deeply for Frank. Even the occasional snicker or kick at a stall partition by a skittish horse didn't disturb him and he might have slept long after the first rising of the sun if the opening of the big doors hadn't permitted the brightness of that early morning to fall directly onto the place where he lay. Even so, his first instinct was to ignore its call to labour, to remain in the arms of Morpheus, and perhaps he would have done so if certain words of a conversation below hadn't penetrated his drowsiness and snapped open his eyes. The words were *Carter Ford* and the manner of their utterance suggested both urgency and conspiracy. With the utmost care, lest his movement should expose his presence, he rolled to the edge of the loft and looked down on the scene below.

The big doors were no more than slightly ajar and the stable, thereby, more in darkness than light but, intermittently, Frank was able to see two men as they passed in and out of shadows. They were busy with the accoutrements for travel, collecting equipment from a saddle rail and using it to harness a horse that had been led from one of the stalls. Silently and secretly, Frank watched their industry trying hard to hear their conversation, because their identities had been revealed by a white hat that shone like a beacon each time it passed through the stream of daylight. In fact, only one of the pair spoke, the man in the blue placket shirt, who seemed to have authority over the other.

'You know where to find Ford,' he said. 'Tell him to forget the raid he had planned for next week. It's not safe for him to cross the river until he hears from me. I'll rub out the fellow who came looking for him at the first opportunity. Meanwhile I'll talk to Adams, try to persuade him to hang around here but he got scared real good last night. He's talking about quitting the town, moving farther west.'

'Do you want me to come back here?'

'No. Stay with Carter and the boys. You'll be needed to drive the next herd.'

The last words were spoken as they left the stable and within a few seconds Frank heard the sound of a horse being ridden away. Swiftly, he descended, saddled his horse and set off in pursuit. It was imperative to catch the man in the white hat. Without his message reaching Carter Ford the raid that was planned would go ahead as scheduled and Frank could have the crews of the Red Diamond and the Wheel ready to apprehend them. Although the man was out of sight by the time Frank left the stable he was certain that he would be riding towards Winter Gulch. Putting spurs to his horse, he raced away from Tomahawk Wells with the utmost determination to close the gap on his quarry.

But his departure was not unobserved. After leaving the stable, the man in the blue shirt had lit a cigarette and leant against a post while the townsfolk began to go about their business. He meant to loiter in the vicinity of the hotel to intercept Foster Adams before he quit town on the morning train. The unexpected sound of the stable doors reopening, however, dragged his attention in that direction. Pete the stableman had not been around when Gil had saddled up and there was no reason for anyone else to be there at that time of the morning. The thought that their conversation had been overheard was troubling but he figured that it was unlikely anyone would tell the sheriff or anyone else about it. Most people attended to their own business and wouldn't interfere in anything that didn't affect them directly. Still, he needed to be sure and watched the rider who emerged from the building at a gallop. Recognition was immediate. He threw aside his cigarette, cursed then hurried back to the stable to saddle his own horse.

Frank had picked up the fresh tracks shortly after leaving Tomahawk Wells. The man in front was travelling fast even though rain was falling once again. Prudence dictated to Frank a need to don his oilskin covering, but he was loathe to relinquish any ground he'd gained so continued through the downpour. He'd been riding for almost an hour before catching the first glimpse of his quarry. Movement, a small dark blur half a mile ahead across the plain, caught his eye. Ignorant of pursuit, the man had obviously taken precautions to keep himself dry and was now wearing a black cape but, even though it was soaked, his white hat was still recognizable.

As his prey disappeared into one of the many dips that abounded in that area, Frank spurred his mount to a fresh effort. Now that he was closing in on the man he had to face the predicament of what to do with him. He had no legal authority to capture him, and even if he had, the jail in Winter Gulch was the last place he wanted him to be held. News of his imprisonment might induce the change to Carter

Ford's plans that he was hoping to avoid. Still, Frank knew he hadn't enough evidence to enforce an arrest in Winter Gulch, especially when the rustling had taken place in another state. The only alternative seemed to be to get him back across the big river to Braceville but that was neither easily accomplished nor legal. He had no actual proof that the man in the white hat had taken an active part in the raids on the Wheel or Red Diamond ranches. But suddenly, all such thoughts became redundant.

The rainfall increased as, following the other man's tracks, Frank went over the lip of a saucer-like hollow. So much had fallen in recent days that the thirty feet descent had become soft and slippery. Consequently, Frank allowed his horse to pick its own line to the bottom, which it did gingerly. The depths of the other horse's tracks made it clear that it, too, had tackled the descent with caution. Unexpectedly, when he reached the bottom, he discovered that his quarry hadn't gone straight across the basin to climb the far bank. Instead, the trail headed away to his left, along the floor of the depression where the bowl narrowed into a tree-lined, narrow channel that twisted away to the north. Frank yelled encouragement to his horse and spurred it forward, picking up such speed that he almost rode past the man sheltering beneath a low cottonwood.

It was the man's horse, shuffling and snuffling as it reacted to the approach of Frank's own animal, which alerted him to the fact that the chase had come to an end. The man in the white hat had dismounted and was in a semi-crouched position trying to light up a freshly made cigarette. Frank's horse slithered to a halt and the men gazed at each other. Recognition of the new arrival came slowly to the man in the white hat, but as his identity became clear so did the knowledge that this wasn't a chance encounter. He'd been pursued to stop him reaching Carter Ford, and with that thought in his mind he reached for his gun. His long cape proved to be a hindrance and before he could draw he became aware that Frank had turned his horse and was now charging in his direction. Taking to his heels, he began to climb the side of the gulch, scrambling and sliding on the wet ground while wending his way between the numerous trees that grew there. He did this not only to eliminate the horse's speed advantage but also to give him protection lest, as he expected, Frank decided to use his gun, too.

It was a good tactic. Frank quickly became aware that, mounted in such trying conditions, he was merely a larger and more cumbersome target to a gunman with a high ground advantage. The man's first shot whistled past Frank's ear and hurried him out of the saddle. His feet slipped as he dismounted and he sank to his knees behind his horse, a manoeuvre that not only provided some protection but also gave him time to study the terrain and try to pinpoint the location of his quarry. A gunfight hadn't figured in his thinking but he wouldn't shirk from it if killing the man was the only way to prevent him delivering his message to Carter Ford.

Another shot rang out, kicking up dirt close to the horse's forelegs. It reared, sprang a couple of steps to the side and would have exposed Frank to the gunman if he hadn't already dived into the cover of some nearby bushes. A wisp of smoke betrayed the white hat's location and Frank fired two shots at the high sycamore that was being used as a shield. Both bullets cleaved bark from the tree. While the man took evasive action to avoid the lead and splinters, Frank sought fresh cover from which to plot a route that would give him an advantage over his opponent.

Three shots lacerated the bush from which Frank had fired, a retaliation that confirmed his belief that the other man thought he was still in that place. Frank also calculated that the man had fired five shots, which probably meant that he'd emptied his revolver. Now, while the man was putting fresh loads in the chambers, Frank seized the opportunity to move again, to get closer to his prey. Already he'd studied the formation of the ground, had noted the curvature of the hillside and had calculated that by means of a circuitous course he might be able to gain the higher ground undiscovered. That would give him an advantage over his opponent. Crawling through the long sodden grass wouldn't be pleasant but he couldn't get any wetter. His clothes were clinging as heavily to him as they would have been if he'd been tipped from his saddle into a river. With a wipe of his hand across his face to clear the rainwater from his eyes, he began his journey.

No more shots were fired as he progressed up the hillside. A need to keep his own movements secret prevented Frank from raising his head to seek out the other's last known location. If he was still by the same tree it was probable that he was scouring the hillside with his eyes to detect some sign of his adversary, or perhaps he believed that his three shot fusillade had been successful, that he'd hit and either killed or wounded his adversary. Frank had no way of knowing, and could only press on with his own stratagem and hope it proved successful.

It took several minutes to reach a point on the hillside that he adjudged higher than his opponent's last known place. Using a tree for cover, he rose to his feet then peered cautiously around. Down below he could see the two horses, steam rising from each as a token of the effort they'd made in the run from Tomahawk Wells. For a long while there was no other movement and Frank began to suspect that while he'd been crawling along the ground his adversary had climbed to the top of the embankment to find either refuge or a suitable place from which to ambush him. But logic told Frank that the man wouldn't go anywhere without his horse; he was the sort of man who wouldn't enjoy being afoot. For a few more seconds he stood motionless against the tree but he knew that eventually it would be necessary to go in search of his prey. The onus was on him to find the man in the white hat and prevent him reaching Carter Ford.

When he did move, when he left the coverage provided by the tree, he almost walked into the man he was seeking. Not ten yards away and unaware of the close proximity of his adversary, the man's back presented a clear target. It took only a moment for Frank to discover that the other's black oilskin had snagged on a long, slender offshoot and he was trying to free himself without giving away his position. Frank had the man at his mercy but killing a man in cold blood was not in his nature.

'Drop the gun,' he said softly.

The man ceased his activity, looked over his shoulder, his face wearing an expression that mirrored his predicament. For a moment it seemed that he was contemplating a continuation of the fight but a gesture by Frank with the cocked gun in his hand convinced him that he had no chance of success. He dropped the gun at his feet.

Once again, Frank was faced with the problem of what to do with his prisoner. 'Free yourself,' he told him, indicating the cape that was attached to the bush.

Unknown to Frank, the man had succeeded in detaching the cape from the offending tendril at the very moment he'd been ordered to drop his gun and now, realizing that his captor thought his movements were restricted, saw a possibility for escape. Frank's eyes were on the discarded gun and he stepped closer to his prisoner to kick it into the undergrowth. Instantly, the man struck, swinging the loose cape, sweeping the gun from Frank's hand and using the same momentum to bundle his body against Frank, effectively knocking him off balance and onto the wet grassy ground.

Aware that he now had an advantage, the man in the white hat made a move to pick up his own gun, but although Frank had been taken by surprise his reaction was instantaneous. He dived forward, grabbed his opponent's legs and sent him sprawling on the ground. The man kicked out and the heavy blow that landed on Frank's chest caused him to release his grip. Again, the man tried to reach his pistol and again Frank responded with swiftness. Jumping on the other's back, he used his knees to drive the air out of his body and dragged his outstretched arm away from the weapon. Turning him over, Frank delivered a blow to his head.

The man was tough and fighting for his life. He jerked his head forward, executing a butt that should have broken Frank's nose but, in pursuance of past investigations, Frank had been involved in brawls from San Francisco's waterfront to mining towns in the Dakotas and read the man's intention before the blow was delivered. Even so, the man's forehead struck his cheek and he was forced to roll away. As he did so, he retained a grip on the man's cape and as he slid downhill he was able to pull the man with him, dragging him away from the place where the pistol lay.

At the end of their slide, both men were breathing heavily. Somehow, the man gained the upper hand, his body pinning Frank to the ground and he was using elbows, knees and any other part of his body that would cause damage or free him from Frank's hold. Although the cape made it difficult for him to engender a full swing of his arms, his legs suffered from no such handicap. A knee jerk caught Frank in the side causing him to gasp. The man saw his opportunity, wriggled free and gained his feet. To give himself time to go back up the hillside for his gun he aimed a debilitating kick at Frank's head. Frank caught the foot before it made contact, twisted and pushed so that his adversary lost balance, fell and slid down the muddy hillside at an accelerating pace.

His collision with a tree brought to an abrupt end the anxious cries of the man in the white hat. When Frank found him almost at the bottom of the slope he knew that he was dead. The man's head was twisted at an unnatural angle to his body; his neck was broken. Frank knelt at his side, his only thought being that the problem of what to do with the man in the white hat was now solved. His way was now clear to return to his uncle and organize a reception posse to capture the rustlers when they made their raid across the river,

Suddenly, a shot rang out and a slug lifted his hat clean off his head. Instinctively, Frank rolled to the side, seeking refuge behind the tree and the body of the man in the white hat. He reached for his sidearm and his hand slapped against an empty holster. Like the dead man's gun, his was somewhere at the top of the hill. Another shot spliced a chunk out the tree. Whoever was shooting at him was using a rifle, thereby banishing all hope of re-climbing the hillside without being hit. His horse, its head lifted in nervous reaction to the gunshots, was at the foot of the hill, less than twenty yards distant, and there was a rifle in the saddle boot. He was weighing his chances of reaching it. Perhaps there were sufficient places that offered cover but he needed to know the gunman's location.

That mystery was solved a moment later when a horseman, rifle in hand, showed himself on the rim at the other side of the basin. Frank recognized him instantly and wasn't surprised to discover that his new assailant was the man in the blue placket shirt. Nor was he surprised when he fired again and again, the bullets chipping great notches out of the tree he was using for protection. Apparently the man was heartened by the lack of return fire because he nudged his horse forward to begin the same descent that Frank himself had made a few minutes earlier. He watched the careful way the horse picked its steps, knew the ground was too treacherous for it to move quickly and decided that this was the only opportunity he would have to reach the saddle gun.

He paused a moment longer, waited until the concentration of the man in the blue shirt was fixed on the trail his horse had chosen, then made a dash for a weapon. A bullet whined past his head, so close that it caused him to lose his balance. He tumbled and rolled the last few feet of the hillside and saw dirt kick up from the ground as another shot was fired in his direction. He was flat on his back now and without hope. His foe was riding towards him, working the mechanism to eject the spent shell and put another cartridge in the breech. He lifted the rifle to his shoulder and squinted along the barrel.

The shot that came was from the slope that Frank had just slid down. The man in the blue placket shirt jerked backwards and his rifle fell from his hands. He crashed to the ground in an ungainly yet unmoving pose.

A horseman emerged from the hillside trees. He slipped his rifle back into its scabbard.

'I hope this has something to do with rustlers,' said Mustang Moore.

SEVEN

Mustang's delayed return to Winter Gulch had been caused by the needs of Meg Rouse and Alice. The rear wheel of the medicine show wagon had collapsed again shortly after crossing the river and the damage was beyond fixing with the knowledge and equipment at Mustang's disposal. So he'd left the womenfolk to camp overnight in the incapacitated vehicle while he continued the journey to Braceville to organise their rescue. That achieved, next day he'd made a beeline for Winter Gulch. Unable to find Frank, his enquiries had eventually led him to the conclusion that he'd gone to Tomahawk Wells. Unsure of his next move he'd hung around Winter Gulch for another day but, bored with inactivity, had set off in pursuit. The sound of gunshots had hurried him to this part of the trail.

After listening to Frank's story, Mustang pointed at the nearby bodies. 'What do we do with those two?'

'That one,' said Frank, indicating the man in the blue shirt who had been blasted out of his saddle, 'we'll hide among those bushes. I don't suppose his body will ever be found.'

When they'd moved it, Frank unsaddled the man's horse and chased it away. It didn't go far, seeking shelter from the rain among the nearby trees.

'What about the other one?' Mustang wanted to know.

Frank had noticed the rowel brand on that man's horse and had begun to wonder about the involvement of the Spur in the rustling of stock from across the river. 'Let's load him onto his horse,' he said. 'I'll take him to the Spur ranch. It'll give me the opportunity to look the place over.'

'What about me?'

'Get back to the Red Diamond without delay. I'll join you there as soon as possible but my uncle must be told that Carter Ford means to strike again soon. Perhaps he's already across the river and hiding out in the hills. My uncle and Willard Draysmith need to be making plans to prevent the loss of more stock.'

'We've got an advantage this time,' Mustang told him. 'All of this rain has swollen the river. With a herd of cattle they won't have any choice but to cross at the island. It'll be impossible anywhere else.'

Those were Mustang's parting words. In an instant, his pony had scrambled up the slippery bank and was gone from Frank's sight. Ensuring that the body he was transporting was securely tied to the horse, Frank soon followed but at a more sedate pace.

Although he didn't know the exact location of the Spur ranch, from overheard conversations and snippets of information he'd picked up in Winter Gulch, Frank knew it lay somewhere to the north of that town. He figured that by drifting in that direction he was sure to meet up with some drovers who would point out the right trail. After an hour in the saddle he came across a large herd, the animals huddled together in defiance of the rain. The outer beasts showed no interest in him as he rode the flank. Up above the cattle, using what shelter could be provided by a low cottonwood, two men watched his approach. They'd dismounted and had stretched their waterproofs over the lowest branches to form a kind of tent. When he reached them their eyes strayed instantly to the bundle carried by the trailing horse. Its brand prompted the question that was asked.

'Who is that?'

'I don't know,' Frank told him. 'Found him back across the range. Recognized the brand. Figured I'd bring him here where he might be known.'

'It's Sour Belly,' the second man said. He'd loosened the ropes so that he could lift the head to see the face.

'Friend of yours?'

'I knew him. What happened?'

'Broke his neck,' Frank said. 'I reckon his horse slipped on a muddy slope back there and threw him. He was dead against a tree at the foot of a bank when I found him.'

'This country,' the man said, retightening the knots. 'Most of the time you can't get enough water to wash the dust out of your throat and think you'll die of thirst. When rain does come along it catches you unawares and kills you before it stops.'

'You want us to take him back to the ranch?' the first man wanted to know.

'If you point out the trail, I'll do it. I don't reckon it'll be far out of my way.'

'If it's work you're seeking there's a full crew at present.'

Frank cast an eye at the bundle on the horse behind. 'There's one vacancy.'

'Yeah, well Sour Belly wasn't a regular hand.'

'Oh! What did he do?'

'Whatever Jake Murdoch told him to do.'

'Is Jake Murdoch the foreman?'

The man didn't answer, turning away to put an end to that conversation.

'Keep that low ridge to your left,' the other one advised. 'It's not more than five miles to the ranch.'

Frank took the hint and gigged his horse forward, moving off at a brisker canter than he'd arrived. It was an unpleasant journey; the heavy clouds darkened the world and violent squalls swept across the range, scrubbing rain into Frank's face with unrelenting ferocity. The horses, too, soon became reluctant to continue but with no place to shelter there was little choice for any of them but to keep moving.

A plateau gave Frank his first sighting of the ranch. Although this represented only a portion of the Spur empire it was a spread that matched in size any cattle ranch he'd ever seen. Nonetheless, he could detect little activity. The dreadful rainfall, it appeared, had driven everyone away from the corrals, pens and outbuildings close to the house. Frank spurred his horse forward and rode down to the gate and into the yard. He hollered for attention.

The man who answered the call beckoned Frank to the stable from which he'd emerged. Even though his movement was minimal and his hat was pulled down low to cheat the still falling rain, Frank found something familiar in his mannerisms. He climbed down and led his horses into the high building. There was a group of men inside all waiting, it seemed, for the rain to cease so they could go about their business. Horses had been saddled and were tethered here and there in readiness for a break in the weather. When Frank removed his hat and shook the water from it onto the floor he sensed a rising interest in his presence.

Looking round he realized that the men were those whose camp he'd stumbled into a couple of nights earlier.

'Well,' said Burt, who had acted as their leader at the first meeting, 'I thought you were going to Tomahawk Wells.'

'Completed my business there,' Frank replied.

'You in the cattle business?'

'What else is there in this part of the country?'

Burt grinned. 'So what brings you here? Sheltering from the rain?'

Frank tugged the lead rein of the trailing horse so that it stepped alongside. 'The horse is Spur stock so I reckoned the rider was too.'

Burt spoke to one of the gathered men. 'Who is it, Clay?'

'It's Gil. Gil Sowerby.'

Five pairs of questioning eyes were fixed on Frank.

'What happened?' Burt asked.

'Way I figured it,' Frank told the men, 'his horse slipped on a muddy bank and the fall killed him.'

Judging by the stern expressions that surrounded him, Frank assumed that his listeners weren't satisfied with that explanation.

Burt said, 'Was he alone?'

'I didn't see anyone else.'

'I thought Gil and Joe were staying in Tomahawk Wells until the beef was shipped out,' Clay said.

'Perhaps something's gone wrong,' said Johnny.

'Perhaps Sour Belly was bringing a message.'

'Shut up,' Burt ordered, and again suspicious eyes were turned towards Frank. 'Step down,' he said, the words reaching Frank's ears as more of a threat than an invitation.

'I'll keep travelling,' he said. 'I can't get any more wet than I am already.'

Frank had noticed the man called Totem on the move, gliding like a shadow out of the range of his vision, edging towards the doors. Still in the saddle, he shortened his rein and pulled, commanding his horse to skip backwards, making it impossible for the mixed-blood to close the doors.

'Besides,' he added, 'you seem ready to hit the trail, too.'

'Yeah, I suppose we are. Could be we're going in the same direction. You didn't say where you were heading.'

'No. I didn't.'

Frank commanded his horse to retreat further so that he was half outside the stable. A voice behind arrested his progress.

'Careful,' the man shouted and Frank realized that he was obstructing the entrance for another horseman. Utilizing the other's arrival to hurry his horse out of the building, Frank turned it, put spurs to its flanks and rode out of the yard. Like everyone abroad in the current wet conditions, the newcomer was covered by his black slicker from neck to saddle and his hat was low on his head so that little of his face could be seen, but Frank had recognized the rider. It was Lou Murdoch. On past occasions when he'd met that young man his older, surlier brother had not been far away. A hint of a feud had been developing between them but this wasn't the time to pursue it. He raced away from the ranch yard before either Jake showed up or the men in the stable decided to mount up and pursue him.

In fact, in the stable, his role in the death of Gil 'Sour Belly' Sowerby had come under discussion when it was discovered that the dead man's pistol wasn't in his holster. Without going in search of it they would never know whether or not their comrade had used it before his death, but no one had ascertained the place where the 'accident' had occurred, so it would probably be a long, fruitless search.

Unlike his volatile brother, Lou Murdoch considered problems before acting and warned against the risk of drawing attention to themselves by acting too hastily.

'Just because he's made an enemy of my brother it doesn't mean he's on a mission to put a stop to our activities, ' he said. 'He saved those women from Jake's temper and, by coincidence, was in the Northern Rose when Buck was killed, but there's no proof that he came to Winter Gulch looking for cattle thieves.'

'Just coincidence, too, that he stumbled into our camp and then turns up here with Sour Belly's body,' argued Burt.

Lou conceded that, at another time, he wouldn't be averse to investigating the man's presence in Winter Gulch, but for the present they were needed across the river. He'd received a message from Jake urging them to join him at their camp in the Comstock Hills.

Burt wasn't happy. Sour Belly hadn't been much of an asset to the gang but his death deserved a bit more attention than it was currently receiving. 'Someone should go to Tomahawk Wells,' he suggested. 'Joe will know the reason for Gil's lone journey.'

'We can't spare anyone,' Lou told him but, relenting a little, told Clay and Will to watch the stranger's movements in Winter Gulch. 'I don't think we have anything to fear from him but take note of who he talks to and where he goes. Meet up with us in the hills tomorrow.'

Burt wasn't as ready as Lou to dismiss the threat that the stranger represented. He'd lived on the wrong side of the law too long to distrust his own instincts and, on both occasions they'd met, the stranger had displayed that mixture of wariness and confidence that he associated with lawmen on the prowl. Perhaps he was wrong, perhaps the man wasn't trying to track down rustlers, but why take the chance? If Carter Ford had been with them the man would not have been allowed to ride away. Bullets would have been pumped into him to ensure he didn't disrupt their plans. But here on the Spur ranch, the Murdoch brothers had been allowed to think they had some influence. Lou's arrival had been at an inopportune moment and the man had taken advantage of the diversion and fled. Burt doubted that such confusion would get the chance to occur again. Jake and Lou Murdoch had been drawn into the enterprise because of their access to Spur equipment and facilities. So far, they had been useful, especially with their knowledge of little used trails to the railhead at Tomahawk Wells, but one was a danger to the continuance of their success because of his temper and the other because he thought he was smarter than he really was. Carter Ford would have to resolve the problem when they all met up at the hill camp.

After quitting the ranch, Frank had ridden south as though Winter Gulch was his destination but his main aim was make a run east for the river and cross it before nightfall. He'd put three miles between himself and the Spur ranch before halting among some hillside trees. He'd ridden with many backward glances in the expectation of sighting horsemen on his trail, knowing that the men in the stable were as suspicious of his story regarding their dead comrade as he was of their involvement of the rustling that was depleting the herds of his uncle and Willard Draysmith. The conversation he'd overheard between Gil Sowerby and Joe in Tomahawk

Wells had linked them directly with the stolen cattle and, subsequently, the brand on Gil's horse had connected him to the Spur organization. Although the cowboys he'd run into before reaching the ranch had known Sour Belly they'd been dismissive of his value as a ranch hand. The men in the stable, however, having identified Gil as one of their crew were clearly surprised that he'd left Tomahawk Wells and it was that surprise that was foremost in Frank's mind. It wouldn't take them long to reach the conclusion that Gil had been the bearer of information that was crucial to their enterprise, and it lodged in his mind that they would want their leader to know of his failed attempt as quickly as possible. Although Burt had assumed the role of leader of the five men he'd twice encountered, Frank was sure he wasn't the ringleader of the outfit. That title, he presumed, belonged to Carter Ford who Gil had been instructed to find. So far, Frank had not met anyone who matched the description he'd been given of that man but perhaps an opportunity to find him would soon present itself. He remembered that the men in the stable had been ready to leave the ranch when he'd arrived with Gil Sowerby's body. Their horses were saddled in anticipation of a cessation of the rain. Perhaps they were merely anxious to savour the pleasures of one of the saloons in Winter Gulch but the possibility also existed that they intended to meet up with their leader.

The downpour had abated. Frank dismounted then removed his hat to shake off the water. He judged himself to be an hour's ride from the big river and the light, which hadn't been good at any time of the day, was dwindling quickly. He knew he couldn't tarry long in this place if he wanted to complete most of the journey to the Red Diamond before total darkness descended. He didn't have Mustang Moore to guide him through the Comstocks' maze of trails.

For several minutes he kept his eyes fixed on the trail he travelled and, just when he was about to remount and ride for the river, his eyes fell on the group of men riding hard in his direction through the murky light. There were six horsemen. Frank recognized Lou Murdoch as the additional rider. He had not expected that young man to be involved with rustling but he would have to pay for his crimes along with his cohorts.

As he watched, two of the riders split away from the remainder. They kept on the southbound trail that led to Winter Gulch. The other four rode east, heading towards the river crossing. Because Foster Adams, the cattle buyer, had been adamant that Carter Ford would soon be driving another herd of cattle to the railroad pens at Tomahawk Wells, it was easy for Frank to surmise that their purpose was once more to raid the herds of the Red Diamond and Wheel ranches. Maintaining a parallel course, he set off in pursuit.

Frank watched their progress but knew his problems would begin at the river. Until then he could remain out of sight; the mud kicked up by their galloping animals produced a track that was easy to follow. Mustang had prophesised that the island would be the only fordable point on the river and the cattle thieves knew it too. From the cover of the bank side trees, Frank watched the men cross, climb away from the river and ride off towards the hills. He waited until he was sure the river was hidden from their sight before following. Although it had only been a few days since he'd made the journey in the opposite direction he was instantly aware of the effect of the incessant rain. The level of the water was higher against his animal's chest and the flow had added strength. He wondered if the rustlers would persist in their raid or if they would be deterred from attempting to drive cattle through such a flood. Such consideration was soon swept from his mind as he set about following the tracks of the men ahead.

The trail was easy to follow but he couldn't rush headlong in their wake. He didn't want to alert them to the fact that someone was on their trail and ride into an ambush. Until the tracks led into a narrow gully the gathering gloom had been his ally, then it added to his discomfort. If the group ahead had discovered that they were being pursued they could be waiting behind any bush, tree or rock to shoot him. He knew his life was forfeit if they caught him but he pressed on. From time to time he halted to listen for the sound of hoof beats but in the low valley the ground was too soft for noise to carry. The only sound was the soughing of the trees that were disturbed by the breeze. The closeness of the surrounding hills decreased the light available and it was yet too soon for the moon to provide any assistance. Frank moved on, at one moment his eyes were searching the ground to confirm he was going in the right direction and the next moment they were peering at every obstacle that could provide cover for a sniper.

It was the close observation of a particularly dense thicket that caused Frank to miss the place where the riders had veered away from the gully. His concentration on the possible threat contained within those high bushes and the need to be ready to react to the presence of a deadly gunman came at the expense of his attention to the ground ahead. Indeed, he was a hundred yards or more beyond that place before he realized his error. When he retraced his steps he found a narrow trail that climbed up into the low hills and followed it. The light of day had almost expired when, from the brow of a hill, he looked down upon a natural bowl of flat land among the surrounding mounds. Two primitive buildings could be seen and horses grazed silently in a nearby corral. Dim light illuminated the windows of one of the buildings and through a tin funnel in the roof, smoke rose. Frank knew he'd found the rustlers' hideout.

A cursory glance told Frank that there were more horses in the corral than the four he'd followed from the Spur. Increasing the crew could have only one motive: a raid on the ranches at this side of the river was imminent. It crossed Frank's mind that it would benefit his uncle and Willard Draysmith if they knew exactly where the rustlers intended to strike. If he got close to the buildings it might be possible to overhear their conversation. Although the increasing darkness seemed to alleviate the necessity to hide his horse, caution had ever been Frank's watchword, so he tethered it among trees while he made his way stealthily downhill.

It wasn't until he reached the corral that he realized that both huts were occupied. He counted eighteen horses, which bespoke a force capable of executing raids simultaneously on Red Diamond and Wheel stock. It also meant that Frank needed to proceed with greater caution if he hoped to eavesdrop on the rustlers. His first object was to reach the cabin from which smoke arose without startling the horse herd. Any sound from them could give warning to the men inside of his presence. Considering the brutal manner in which they had slaughtered the Red Diamond riders during their last raid, he knew he could expect no mercy from them if caught spying.

The cabin from which smoke arose was his prime target but that one was furthest from the corral. He had no idea if he would be able to hear with clarity anything of the conversation taking place inside, nor, if he could, if he would learn anything of the gang's plans, but it was an opportunity he couldn't ignore. Keeping low, he ran from the corral to the nearest hut. Within, he could hear the mumble of voices and the sound of a harmonica. He edged around a corner, which brought him to the rear of the building. Lights glowed in the windows and he crawled under them to the far corner where he paused briefly before making a dash for the rear of his target hut.

Halfway between, the door of the building behind opened. Words spilled into the night, laughter accompanied them and Frank fell flat on his face and remained motionless while a man cast the dregs from a coffee pot on the ground, spat, and then went back inside. The incident had lasted less than a minute but it had been long enough to press home to Frank the tenuous thread that existed between safety and discovery. Swiftly, he regained his feet and finished his run, slipping into the shadows provided by the other building. Again, he crept along the rear of the building, removing his hat before risking a quick glance through a window. That room was in darkness so he moved on, circumnavigating the hut until he'd reached the front.

Kneeling, he peered inside and counted eight men, the majority of whom were gathered around a small table with cards in their hands. Lou Murdoch was amongst their number but his brother was at the far side of the room, his chair balanced on its rear legs so that his back rested against the wall. He was scanning a catalogue with the avid intent of a man eager to spend money. It was the remaining occupant, however, who held Frank's attention. He was a tall man in a long, fringed buckskin coat and when he turned away from the stove where he'd been filling his cup from a coffeepot, Frank was able to see the slim beard at the point of his chin. Frank had found Carter Ford, the man responsible for the slaying of the Red Diamond riders.

That sighting satisfied Frank's curiosity. There was no need to risk lingering around the cabins any longer. Carter Ford's presence was an assurance that a raid was imminent. Gingerly, Frank retraced his route around the huts, past the corral and up the hillside to the place where his horse patiently awaited his return. He'd taken barely a couple of strides down the far side of the hill when he heard the jingle of harness coming towards him. He steered his mount back among the trees hoping to avoid discovery. Even so, a voice, tense, challenged him.

'Who's that?'

'What is it?' another man asked.

'Thought I saw someone up ahead,' he was told.

Among the trees, Frank drew his gun. He didn't want to use it, didn't want to announce his presence to those in the cabins below, but he would defend himself if it became necessary. He waited.

The second voice betrayed its owner's reluctance to believe they were under any kind of threat. 'I don't see anything.'

'There was someone there, I tell you.'

Frank heard the sound of a long gun being slid out of its saddle boot.

'What are you doing, Will?'

'I'll put some bullets into those bushes. That'll flush out whoever's there.'

'Don't be a fool,' the other said. 'It'll be a bear or an antelope, something living in the wild. You don't want everyone to know you're shooting at shadows. Burt won't be happy that we couldn't find that stranger in Winter Gulch; we don't want to give him anything else to grumble at us about.'

'Nothing we could do about that, Clay. We couldn't find him if he wasn't there.'

'Won't stop him blaming us. Come on, let's get down there.'

Frank heard one horse move forward, saw it move slowly past the place where he watched anxiously lest his own horse should move or snort or in some way signal its presence to the other men's animals. But it was still, and when Will followed his companion to the buildings below, Frank tugged its ears gratefully, but remained hidden until the men had unsaddled their mounts and gone indoors. Then he set course for his uncle's ranch.

EIGHT

Both rider and horse were exhausted when Frank eventually reached the Red Diamond. The place was in darkness, everyone asleep, fostering in him a reluctance to disturb his uncle up at the house. Instead, after stabling his mount, he found a spare place in the bunkhouse and was asleep instantly. The discordant clang of the cook's triangle, the call to breakfast, woke him less than three hours later and he cursed in unison with most of the crew as he lifted his head from the mattress and pulled on his boots.

'When did you get in?' Mustang Moore asked.

'I don't know,' Frank replied honestly, and his head remained fuzzy until he'd dipped it in a bowl of cold water.

He ate with the crew before he and Mustang went up to the house. Titus told his nephew that in response to the urgency in the message that

109

Mustang had brought the previous day, he'd orga-
nized a meeting with Willard Draysmith.

'Are you going out to the Wheel?'

'No. Willard keeps a room at the hotel in town.
I'll join him there around midday.'

'I'll get cleaned up and come with you,' Frank
said.

Later, when he'd washed, brushed and scrubbed the
mud from his horse, his equipment and his own
hair, body and clothes, he'd returned to the stable
to saddle up his horse for the ride into Braceville. A
scuffling, rattling sound drew his attention to the
high, open door. A shadow preceded the person
who limped awkwardly inside.

Frank greeted the young man. 'Good to see you
up and about, Linc,' he said.

The need to regain his breath prevented an
immediate response from Linc Bywater. There was
rigidity about the movement of his upper torso that
bespoke tight bandaging beneath his thick, woollen
shirt. His eyes were deep sunk in his colour-drained
face that, if not a sign that he was struggling against
pain, was indicative of the toll the effort of movement was taking on his strength. He leant against a
stall post while Frank continued fixing the bridle on
his horse's head.

'There's talk in the bunkhouse about another
raid by the rustlers, Mr Sawyer. Is it true?'

'Probably.'

'And you mean to fight them?'

'We'll try to stop them taking any more Red Diamond cattle, Linc, and hopefully persuade them not to come back here.'

'I want to be part of it, Mr Sawyer. I owe them for what they've done to me and to those that were killed up in the hills.'

'Your first job is to get fit again.'

'I'll be fit enough to fight. I can pull the trigger of my rifle as well as any man.'

'I'm sure you can, Linc, and I understand how you feel, but we don't know where or when the attack will come and when it does we'll have to ride hell-for-leather for the river. At the moment I don't think you're able to sit a horse let alone keep up the pace.'

Although hurt by Frank's honest assessment, Linc Bywater was defiant. 'I won't let anyone down again.'

'Far as I know,' said Frank, tightening the cinch, 'you haven't let anyone down yet. In fact it was the information you gave me that put me on the right track. You've done your bit, Linc.'

Linc Bywater pushed himself away from the post. 'I mean to be there, Mr Sawyer. When the fight starts I'll be there.'

Mustang Moore nudged Frank as they rode into Braceville and inclined his head towards the far side of the street. A wagon had been pitched in a gap between two of the town's older buildings, its tailgate lowered to form a small platform. A large board propped against a wheel proclaimed coffee was available for ten cents and pies for twenty. Two or three men near at hand were sampling the offerings. A movement inside the body of the wagon caught Frank's attention and he watched as a familiar figure emerged, a coffeepot in hand to refill the vessel of one of her customers.

'That's Meg Rouse,' he said.

'We should visit while we're in town,' said Mustang, who had twisted in his saddle in order to lift a hand in greeting when eventually he caught the woman's eye.

The words had been meant for Frank's ears but it was Titus Sawyer who responded. 'We're here to meet up with Willard Draysmith,' he said, 'and to hatch a plan to put an end to the raids on our herds.'

His nephew wasn't likely to forget their reason for coming to town. He'd spent an exhausting few days on the other side of the big river seeking information about the rustlers but he'd also provided aid to the stricken women in the medicine show wagon. In his opinion, saying hello to them was nothing more than the neighbourly thing to do. Still, they rode on to the hotel where they'd arranged to meet the owner of the Wheel but, when they learned that Willard Draysmith hadn't yet arrived in Braceville, he and Mustang walked back to the roadside coffee stall while Titus went to quench his own thirst in Al Tasker's Diamond Queen.

'We've taken Mr Moore's advice,' said Meg Rouse, bestowing a look on Mustang that made Frank ponder the nature of the relationship that had formed between them. 'Without the Colonel's guidance and protection Alice and I are unable to continue with the show. Therefore we mean to give the good people of Braceville the opportunity to form the same favourable opinion of our cooking as you and Mr Moore so generously conveyed.'

'Won't you need somewhere for them to sit?' observed Frank.

'Indeed,' replied Meg Rouse. 'We've taken a lease on that building,' she pointed to her right, 'but until it's ready for business we thought we'd sell coffee and pies from the wagon. Let the townspeople and ranch-hands know what they can look forward to when we open our eatery.'

'Well, I wish you luck,' said Frank.

'You will come, won't you?' said Alice, rendering a coy smile.

'If I'm still around when you open I'll be your first customer.'

Frank tipped his hat to the women and then, followed reluctantly by Mustang Moore, crossed the street towards the Diamond Queen. Along the boardwalk, the saloon their destination too, hurried two people he recognized. Doctor Theo Jones, Gladstone bag carried in his right hand, led the way towards the swing doors.

'Trouble, Doctor?' asked Frank.

'A matter of life and death,' replied the other, tetchily, as seemed to be his usual manner. 'If I don't get a drink quickly I shall die of thirst.'

'Let me buy you one,' said Frank, but his words were delivered to the doctor's back as the medic brushed aside the batwings and strode into the saloon.

Frank grinned wryly and addressed the person who had been struggling to keep pace with the doctor. 'Must be a man with an almighty thirst,' he said.

Lulu's lips twitched. It was an acknowledgement of Frank's observation but dismissive of the possibility of humour. She would have walked past without comment if Frank hadn't spoken again.

'Are you assisting the doctor now?'

Lulu stopped and turned with an incredulous expression on her face. 'That would put an end to his career in this town,' she said. 'Not only would the good ladies of Braceville stop consulting him but they would insist that their husbands, too, found a different source for the treatment of their ailments.'

'I didn't mean to cause offence,' Frank said, 'but you did a good job with young Linc. That's not just my opinion; Doctor Jones agrees.'

'I did nothing but carry soup,' she said.

Frank knew she'd done more than that. She'd sat with him, sometimes through the night and nursed him through a fever. He didn't know why she'd undertaken the task but she'd shown an aptitude that deserved encouragement.

'Well, it was good soup,' he said. 'It's got him on his feet already and he's talking about fighting the rustlers when we catch up with them.'

'No,' she said, almost violently. 'No. He's not yet fit enough to ride. He lost a lot of blood, a lot of strength. It'll take time for him to recover fully.'

'That's what I told him but he won't listen to me. Perhaps he'll listen to you. Come out to the ranch and visit with him if you want to.'

Again the look of disbelief settled on her face. 'You don't know your uncle very well, do you?'

Frank didn't give voice to any answer but had to confess to himself that her observation was true. Apart from the letters his father received he knew very little about Titus Sawyer.

'He'd be worried that his cattle would be contaminated if I went within spitting distance of the Red Diamond,' she said.

Frank wanted to protest against such a suggestion but the ferocity of her allegation told him that she was surer of her facts than he was.

Then the frowns on her face eased. 'Besides,' she continued, 'the young fellow wouldn't want me turning up. He didn't even know I was around when I was putting the soup spoon to his mouth.'

'Well, I knew you were around and that he wouldn't be so far along the road to recovery if you hadn't been prepared to nurse him.'

'The doctor cured him,' she said.

'But he needed your help. He's been paid for what he did and I'd like to do the same for you.'

'Why?'

'Because you earned it.'

'I'd only waste it on whiskey and laudanum. That's what women like me do.'

Frank had no way of knowing the events that had brought her to this place but, despite her best efforts, he didn't want to believe her. There was a quality to her mannerisms that mismatched the brusqueness and aggression of her words. 'Look, Miss . . . er—'

'Lulu,' she said.

'It's Lulu in there,' he said, motioning with his head to the interior of the Diamond Queen 'but I'm sure you have another name outside.'

'In this town it's Lulu everywhere.'

'Then why don't you leave? Let me buy you a ticket out of here.'

She smiled. It was almost genuine. 'No, Mr Sawyer, no need for you to be concerned about me. I do what I do. Nothing will change that. Can't all find respectability in a new town. Her gaze was directed over his shoulder.

Frank turned his head in the direction of the wagon. Alice was watching them.

'Even a hurdy-gurdy dancer thinks herself superior to me.'

Lulu walked away into the saloon and Frank would have followed if, at that moment, Willard Draysmith hadn't ridden into town.

Until he had both ranchers in the same room, Frank had kept to himself the fact that he'd discovered the rustlers' hideout. He'd anticipated their reaction to the revelation and didn't want to fight off the same argument twice.

'Why didn't you tell me earlier?' asked his uncle.

'Let's roundup some men and storm that place,' said Willard Draysmith.

Frank preached patience. 'Right now they'll be spread across the range, looking for likely herds they can run into the hills. If we go now we might catch a couple in their lair but not necessarily the leaders.'

'Then we surround the place,' interrupted Willard Draysmith. 'Wait until they're all in the valley then attack.'

'They won't surrender without a fight,' Frank told him, 'and there are enough men in that gang to withstand a lengthy siege. Chances are that you'll lose as many men as they do.'

'What do you suggest, Frank?' asked his uncle.

'The way I see it, we can't prove they are rustlers unless we catch them with stolen cattle.'

'Linc Bywater can identify them from the last raid,' said Titus Sawyer.

'At best, Linc can identify one man: Carter Ford.

117

I saw him at the hideout last night but if he's no longer there we have no proof that the others are rustlers and any attack on them would put us outside the law.'

'That's nonsense,' blustered his uncle.

'In spirit, I agree with you,' Willard told Titus, 'but I understand Frank's meaning. If we intend leading our men into battle we don't want them facing charges of unlawful killing in its aftermath.'

'So we've got to let them steal our cattle first!' There was an edge of disbelief to Titus Sawyer's exclamation.

'Because of the weather,' Frank told him, 'the only place to cross the boundary river is at the point where the island has formed midstream. To reach that place from their hideout they must drive the cattle through a narrow gorge. We can trap them there. They'll surrender or die.'

'Let them steal our cattle!' Titus said again, clearly appalled by such a notion.

'You've obviously given this a great deal of thought,' Willard said to Frank. 'Whose cattle do you propose should be stolen?'

'Because of the size of the gang I think they'll be eager to take stock from the rangeland of both the Red Diamond and Wheel. Each of you move a herd of a tempting size close to the hills with only a couple of herders to guard it. Hopefully, the weather will again be helpful to us, causing the rustlers to assume that everyone else is sheltering

118

from the rain. Tell your men not to resist when the attack comes but to report back to the ranch as quickly as possible.'

'You're sure we'll catch them before they cross the river?'

'They'll work on disguising the brand before taking the stock onto Spur land. They won't want to run the risk of running into anyone of authority while in possession of a mixed herd of Red Diamond and Wheel cattle. No, they'll take them back to the hideout valley first, but we know they mean to move them on to Tomahawk Wells as quickly as possible. That'll give us a couple of days to organise the trap.'

NINE

During the course of the following day, four hundred cattle were moved onto Red Diamond pasture between Beaver Creek and the Comstock Hills and further north a smaller herd of Wheel stock was similarly left to graze close to the high ground. Meanwhile, Frank Sawyer guided his uncle, Willard Draysmith, and Mustang Moore to the valley along which the cattle would eventually be driven to the river crossing. Its suitability as a place of entrapment was obvious to all. Certain passages were steep sided and narrow and the whole length was a series of turns that would necessarily impose a gentle pace on the herd.

Although they didn't follow it, Frank pointed out the track that led to the rustlers' hideout.

Willard Draysmith expressed the opinion that the rustlers wouldn't use it to bring the cattle out of the hills. Titus Sawyer agreed.

'Perhaps there is another route to the river from

their hideout,' he said. 'What makes you sure they'll come this way?'

'They're holed up in a closed draw. Without climbing the surrounding hills there is only one route in and out and that trail eventually links into this valley. It puts several miles on their journey but they'll be able to keep control of the herd all the way to the river. Otherwise, they'd be chasing strays all over the hills.'

Satisfied that they could organize the capture of the rustlers in this valley, they selected the place they considered most suitable for the confrontation. It was close to the river end of the valley, which the men from the ranches could approach via other routes from north and south. Here, the trail narrowed to a width that would barely permit the passage of six beasts and the slopes abounded in suitable cover to affect an ambush. Escape for the rustlers would be impossible.

As Frank had suspected, the cattle left near the high ground were found by members of the rustler gang and, later that night in the outlaw's hideaway, the task of running them into their secluded valley was under discussion.

Burt was urging instant action, arguing that the lax guard on the cattle indicated that the ranchers weren't expecting another raid, that they wouldn't expect the rustlers to risk capture following the ambush of the Red Diamond crew on their last

spree. His words were listened to without con-
tention; indeed they were nothing more than an
echo of Carter Ford's own sentiments that had been
used to persuade everyone that an early return to
this side of the river would be another success. The
money that still jingled in their pockets from the
sale of the last herd assured them of their leader's
competence in such matters.

'And the weather,' Burt continued, 'no one wants
to be nursing cows in all this rain. But it can't last
much longer and when the sun comes out there will
be more riders on the range. So let's do it tomorrow.
We can gather in those seven- or eight-hundred
head while the few men that have been left to guard
them are trying to keep dry under canvas sheets.
We'll have the cattle into the hills and into this
valley before their minders get their saddles on
their horses.' He looked around the room for dissenters to his proposal. When no one spoke he
grinned before addressing them again. 'One thing
is certain: they won't try to follow us this time.'

The men in the room waited for their leader to
speak. He was the one who would decide when and
where they struck. Carter Ford had been busy with a
cigarette while listening to Burt. He lit it then blew
out smoke before responding.

'Could be a trap,' he said.

'A trap!' Burt was surprised by the suggestion.

'The ranchers know that their stolen stock is
being run into the hills so why put it in such a handy

spot for us?'

'They're big ranches for this part of the territory,' Burt told him, 'but they still need to use every blade of grass they own. The cattle's there because the grass is good on that stretch.'

'Could be,' Carter Ford agreed, 'but I've got an awful itch in the gut about it.'

'You said it yourself, Carter, these folks don't expect us ever to return here. Probably think we've run all the way to Mexico.' Burt laughed again, casting glances at the other men in search of support.

'Yeah,' said the leader, 'that was the way we figured it and there's no real reason to believe any different now, but if these ranchers ever catch us they'll have no mercy. They'll hang every one of us. Let's be cautious.'

A hush fell on the room. It was Burt, of course, who broke the silence. 'What are we going to do?' he asked.

'If the ranchers have something planned they won't be able to keep it secret. Jake,' Carter Ford called to the elder Murdoch, 'I want you an' Clay to hang around Braceville tomorrow. Keep your eyes and ears open. Get back here quickly if you discover anything that suggests a trap.'

Later, when they were alone, Burt had raised his concerns with regard to the Murdoch brothers. Carter Ford eased his mind.

'We no longer have any need of them,' he assured

his second-in-command. 'After this run we'll stay well away from this part of the territory. Some people I spoke to in Tomahawk Wells spoke of large herds further west.' He grinned slyly at the other. 'Too many cattle on the range doesn't give the grass a chance to grow.'

'Yeah,' said Burt, 'we're doing the nation a favour by thinning down the herds.'

'Reckon the Spur itself has too many cattle,' said Carter Ford 'but it doesn't seem right to involve the Murdoch boys in raids against their employer.'

'What do you mean to do?'

'After we've got the next herd over the river they can go back to the Spur. I'll tell them they'll get their share after the beef has been shipped out of Tomahawk Wells.'

'But they'll have a long wait!'

'They'll have a very long wait.'

It was after noon the following day when Frank Sawyer drove a buckboard into Braceville. Alongside him sat Linc Bywater who, before the outset, had insisted he was capable of riding into town and for most of the journey had grumbled about being treated like a sick schoolboy when he was as fit as any man on the ranch. Without passing comment, Frank noticed how every unexpected bump and bounce made his passenger wince.

'When the doc says you're fit for work again, I'm sure my uncle will have you back in the saddle,' he said, but added, 'don't expect that to be today.'

Because of the heavy rain, the approach road into town was churned into a morass of mud and puddles. Braceville's main street, too, was a mire through which the horses would have difficulty pulling the wagon. Consequently, Frank steered into a large barn that was attached to the livery stable and then left the animals in the care of the stableman while he and Linc went about their business.

They parted company at the home of Doctor Jones, Linc going inside with a grumpy reluctance while Frank continued along the boardwalk. His first stop was the telegraph office to check for messages from his partner in San Francisco, but there were none to collect. Rain was falling again when he left that office and his sudden emergence caused a minor collision between himself and three women. They were hurrying to find a refuge from the downpour and their visibility was restricted by the shawls they'd pulled over their lowered heads for protection. It wasn't until he'd offered his apologies that he recognized the threesome as working girls from the Diamond Queen, one of whom was Lulu. While the other two continued on their way, Frank detained Lulu with the information that Linc was with Doctor Jones.

Once again her response reflected an anger that took Frank by surprise.

'What do you think I'm going to do, Mr Sawyer?

Rush along there with some expectation that he'll see me as the angel of his dreams and whisk me away from a dreary life in a dreary town?'

'I thought you might want to see how well your patient has progressed.' The recollection that the patient had barely stopped grumbling since returning to the Red Diamond jumped to the front of his mind but Linc's abrasiveness, Frank hoped, was reserved solely for those he held responsible for confining his activities to petty duties around the ranch house.

'No doubt I'll discover how well he's doing one night when his belly's full of whiskey and he has a dollar to spare. Whatever you're expecting to happen, Mr Sawyer, won't.'

'I'm not expecting anything,' he told her. 'You did a good deed and he should be made aware of that.'

The look Lulu cast at him was almost derisory, as though he was too naive to warrant her attention. She turned and began to walk away.

'I suppose, ' Frank said, 'I'm simply interested in knowing why you did it, why you dedicated yourself to his care but now want to wash your hands of the affair.'

When she turned around the harsh expression that had been on her face had slipped away. She paused for a moment then stepped close to him again. 'We all have a story, Mr Sawyer, but if it stops you pestering me I'll tell you part of mine. I came out west to marry a soldier but by the time I reached the fort he'd died of a fever. His dying had been a lengthy, lonely affair and I've always regretted the fact that I didn't arrive in time to comfort him. They said the boy was dying. I didn't want him to be alone. That's it. I did it for my own benefit, to ease my own conscience.'

Frank didn't know how much, if any, of what she'd told him was the truth, but said, 'No need to act like it's something to be ashamed of. Think again about leaving here, perhaps study to be a nurse. It's a good thing to give comfort to the sick.'

'Yeah,' she said, 'I know. I already give comfort to men doing my job at the Diamond Queen. Sometimes they don't appreciate it but I don't suppose that life is perfect for anyone.' Again her expression changed, as though she couldn't decide whether Frank Sawyer was someone she could like or someone whose motives she feared. 'Let me get on with my life, Mr Sawyer, and I won't intrude in yours.'

When she walked away she did so at an unhurried pace, dismissive of the rain that was falling heavily. She didn't look back and didn't stop until she'd reached the boardwalk of the Diamond Queen. A feminine shriek caused her to pause, her attention drawn to something at the other side of the street. Frank, too, heard the shout and like the few other people who were abroad in the rain, turned his steps in that direction.

*

Jake Murdoch and Clay had arrived in town a couple of hours earlier. They'd spoken with the stableman when they first hit town before spending time in the barber's shop where men often gossiped while being attended to with scissors, foam and razor. They overheard nothing that gave cause for suspicion: the unusual weather and the need to create street crossings with planks proved to be the central topics of most conversations. They loitered near the newspaper office where four of the older citizens were engaged in games of checkers until the rain began to fall again. At that point the seniors sprang up like juveniles and hurried away to their own homes. The hotel foyer was too small for Jake and Clay to hang around unobtrusively so, when they saw four cowboys ride in with the Wheel brand on their animals, they hurried down to the Diamond Queen to eavesdrop on their conversation.

Like the townspeople, the newly arrived ranch-hands were full of curses for the continuous rain. No one could recall such a long wet spell and all vowed they would be pleased when they were burning once more under a cruel sun.

'There's nothing to keep us here,' said Clay. Jake had his eyes fixed on a saloon girl who was talking to a man at an adjoining table.

'Forget it,' Clay told him. 'Drink up and we'll

report back. My guess is that we'll be working tonight.'

From a sheltered part of the boardwalk outside the Diamond Queen they watched the scurrying townspeople and studied the rain. They weren't eager to return to the hideout while the rainfall was so heavy. With little sign of improvement, however, they saw no advantage in delay and would have quit town if a glance across the street hadn't revealed something of interest to Jake.

The wagon that had been backed into a space between two buildings was familiar to him. The fancy lettering on the side was impossible to read at the angle from which he viewed it but he already knew what it said: Colonel Abraham Potter's Medicine Show. In verification, a slim figure stepped down from the lowered tailboard and hurried into the nearest building.

'Well, well,' he said with quiet menace.

'What is it?' asked Clay.

'Wait here,' Jake answered and stepped down into the mud and crossed the nearly deserted street.

Squeezing himself between the wagon and the building he waited. When Alice stepped outside he reached out a hand and grabbed her arm. The yell that was forming in his mouth was meant to herald the success of his capture but it turned into a howl of agony. Alice had been carrying a pot of freshly brewed coffee and it flew into the air when Jake seized her arm. Its contents scalded the left side of his face and burned into his eye.

The unexpected attack had wrenched a squeal from Alice, too, a mixture of surprise and pain from the vice-like grip by which she was held. As Jake rubbed his face with the heel of one hand, Alice tried to shake herself free of the other. Jake clung on and jerked hard, almost pulling her off her feet as she stumbled against him.

'Not this time,' he snarled.

Voices were being raised by townspeople who were becoming aware of the incident. Street fights were no more uncommon in Braceville than they were in any similar town in the west. Disputes between men were usually bypassed with barely a glance from the citizens, but this was different. The young woman presented a slight form against the man's bulk and when he thrust her aside it was with such strength that she was unable to prevent herself crashing against one of the wagon's wheels. She fell heavily to the ground.

Ignoring the protests and calls for the sheriff to be brought from his office, Jake leant over Alice. 'I haven't forgotten that you wanted to use a whip on me the last time we met,' he growled. 'Well, it's payback time, and no one here will come to your rescue this time.' He drew his hand back to deliver an open-handed slap.

Frank caught Jake's hand at the top of its swing and pulled him away from his intended victim. 'We've been in this situation before,' said Frank, who then threw a punch that connected with the other's jaw. Jake staggered back a couple of steps but didn't go down. Instead, he lowered his head and charged bull-like at Frank. Frank tried to sidestep but wasn't quick enough. Jake's shoulder caught him in the midriff and they fell in a heap on the ground.

Tussling, each tried to gain the upper hand, neither able to free their arms sufficiently to deliver a blow that was capable of hurting or rendering the other incapable of continuing the fight. The slimy mud in which they wrestled was also a hindrance, causing both men to slip at vital moments when they felt that dominance was within their grasp. It was mud, however, that brought the fight to a conclusion. Supine and his strength waning, Jake filled his hand with mud and thrust it into Frank's face. With a screwing motion, he pushed the wet earth into nostrils and mouth, forcing Frank off his chest. As he tried to clear his breathing passages, Frank was hit by a thunderous punch that almost took away his senses. He rolled, spitting the mud from his mouth, needing to get air into his lungs but aware that another attack was only a moment away.

With Frank on his knees, Jake saw his opportunity for victory. He gained his feet without slipping and aimed at kick at Frank's head. In the nick of time, Frank reacted in an unexpected manner. Simultaneously swallowing and spitting out mud he lunged towards his opponent, his full body colliding with Jake's standing leg before the kick could be delivered. Jake went down again. Despite his handicapped breathing, Frank followed up his attack with a punch that landed solidly on Jake's jaw. Jake slumped in the mud and lay still.

With the aid of the wheel, Frank pulled himself upright then leant against the wagon while he tried to blow the dirt from his nose. He should have remembered Jake's reaction a few days earlier when bested by Mustang but it took a sudden shout to alert him to the danger. If Jake's shot had been accurate, the warning would have been too late but the bullet struck the wheel as Frank began to turn his body. Instinctively, he reached for the gun at his side but the mud on his hands made it difficult to grasp. Before he could pull it from its holster his adversary had fired again. Later, Frank could only assume that mud had been the cause of Jake's second miss but he didn't give him a third chance. He pulled the trigger of his Colt twice and Jake's body jumped as each slug struck home.

Men were standing around in silence and Meg Rouse had an arm around Alice by the time Frank's breathing was unhindered by mud. A voice, loud and important, carried along the street.

'What's this all about, Mr Sawyer?' Sheriff Hayes was marching up the middle of the street, gun in hand. 'I thought I made it clear to you and your uncle that I don't like gunplay in this town.'

'Self-defence, Sheriff; he fired first.'

Frank's version of events was corroborated by witnesses, and Alice added her own story as proof that Jake Murdoch had been the aggressor.

'So he's not one of the rustlers you're after,' said Fred Hayes. When Frank didn't answer he spoke again. 'Are you going to tell me what the Wheel and Red Diamond are cooking up?'

'I don't know what you mean.'

'I saw Titus and Willard Draysmith in town together two days ago,' Fred Hayes said. 'Those two don't meet up here in Braceville unless there's something big to discuss.'

Again Frank remained silent but Alice, who had come to stand at his side while he was being questioned by the lawman, tugged at his sleeve.

'Your girlfriend wants you,' she said.

Frank turned and saw Lulu beckoning from outside the Diamond Queen. He didn't know why Alice had referred to Lulu as his girlfriend but people often had unfathomable thoughts in their head. He'd long since stopped trying to understand them. Trudging through the mud, he crossed the street to the Diamond Queen.

'That man,' she said, indicating a figure who was entering the livery stable, 'I think he was with the man you killed.'

The news that Jake hadn't come to Braceville alone didn't surprise Frank but he asked what reason she had for that belief.

'He was standing near when I shouted the

warning,' she said. 'Judging by the look he gave I think he would have killed me if no one else had been around.'

'You shouted the warning!'

'I figured you would have done the same for me.'

He grinned. 'I'm pleased you've reached the conclusion that I'm not your enemy.' He looked up the street towards the stable. 'Was there anything else that made you suspicious?'

'It could have been a coincidence,' she said, 'but he seemed to take to his heels when the sheriff called you Mr Sawyer.'

Just then a rider emerged from the stable and rode right past Frank and Lulu, who'd moved to a less obtrusive place on the boardwalk. Frank got a clear view of the man's face, knew him as Clay and realized that his association with the Red Diamond had been revealed.

'Is he one of the rustlers?' asked Lulu.

'He is,' said Frank, aware that he must now act quickly.

TEN

Under the conditions, Clay Johnson's approach to the rustlers' hideout was reckless. His horse was exhausted having been urged on with leathers and spurs since quitting Braceville, and now, weary-legged, it slithered on the wet, muddy slope that led to the cabins below.

Will Cassidy, watching from a window, alerted those who were inside. 'Something's wrong,' he drawled. 'Clay's coming in like he's got a Cheyenne war party on his tail.' He went to the door and opened it as Clay jumped clear of his saddle.

Rainwater running off his hat, Clay looked around the room. Every man was waiting for him to speak but he remained silent until his eyes met those of Carter Ford. 'It's a trap, alright,' he said.

'What's happened?' the leader wanted to know.

'The man who brought in Sour Belly's body was in Braceville and I reckon he'd been across the river looking for us or the stolen cattle.'

Carter Ford almost scoffed, as though Clay was

jumping at shadows. 'Is that based on something more than a sighting in town?'

Clay nodded. 'His name is Sawyer and the owner of the Red Diamond is his uncle.'

Ford showed a little more interest. 'Are you sure?'

'I heard the sheriff talking to him, wanting to know what the Red Diamond was cooking up with the Wheel.'

'Did you find out?'

'No. I raced back here with the news.'

'Did Jake stay in town?' asked Lou Murdoch.

'Your brother's dead,' Clay replied without any feeling. 'Sawyer shot him.'

This news piqued Carter Ford's interest. 'What did they fight over?' he wanted to know. 'The theft of the cattle?'

'A girl,' said Clay, who then related the incident that had led to Jake's death.

Lou and his Spur companions were familiar with Jake's proclivities but Carter Ford's brutal assessment that his lack of self-control was always going to get him killed didn't sit easily with them. Edginess crept into the mood of the men in the room. Almost mockingly, Clay Johnson asserted that they were indebted to Jake's recklessness for providing the information he'd gathered.

'We'd learned nothing up to that point,' he said, 'and were preparing to leave town.'

'So no one associated him with stolen cattle,' opined Carter Ford.

'I'm not sure. The way they faced up to each other gave the impression they'd met before.'

'What about you, anyone see you together?'

'Sure, we were in town a couple of hours. We'd followed some Wheel riders into the Diamond Queen to listen to their talk but we didn't do anything to draw attention to ourselves. Not until the fight, but I kept well clear of that and nobody tried to stop me leaving town after Jake was killed.'

For a moment, Carter Ford pondered on the situation. 'I see no reason to abandon our plan,' he said eventually.

Clay pointed out that although nothing specific linked Jake to the rustling he was still convinced that the ranchers had a scheme in place to capture them. 'Those herds we've seen must be some kind of lure to trap us.'

'They'd have to have an army waiting in the hills,' Carter Ford said. 'Has anyone seen any heavily-armed men around here?' The lack of response encouraged him to speak again. 'Let's do it,' he said. 'We can make the raids tonight and have the cattle hidden in this valley long before daybreak. We fooled them once when they tried to follow and we can do it again.'

'We won't be able to raise dust this time,' Burt announced with a look towards the rain-streaked window that brought chuckles from some others.

Lou Murdoch wasn't laughing. 'My brother's been killed,' he said. 'I've no interest in rustling

137

cattle. I'm heading back across the river.'

His intention was echoed by the other Spur riders who had been tempted to ride with the rustlers; their loyalty was to the Murdoch brothers. The death of one, the avowed intent of the other to quit and the threat of capture by vengeful ranchers were sufficient grounds to return to cattle pushing on the Spur side of the river. They hadn't been involved in the massacre that had been perpetrated on the last raid but, nonetheless, they would hang for it if they fell into Red Diamond hands.

'Your brother,' Carter Ford declared, not wanting to deplete his force by the loss of the Spur riders, 'was killed by a Sawyer. Taking their cattle might not be full revenge but you can't let Jake's death go unpunished. Even now, the Sawyers are probably celebrating. You can be sure there won't be anything but the lightest guard on the cattle tonight. We'll have them hidden in this valley before the Red Diamond riders are out of their bunks in the morning. Revenge, Lou. You've got to get revenge for Jake.'

Burt spoke up, echoing his leader's words and putting a question mark against Lou's bravery if he returned to the Spur knowing the identity of his brother's killer but having done nothing to avenge his death.

Lou wasn't going to be buffaloed into acting against his wishes. He'd stood up for his elder brother when he was alive; he saw no value in

138

risking his life or those of his Spur friends now that Jake was dead.

'We're going,' he told Carter Ford and his men gathered together their belongings.

'We'll carry out the raids on our own,' Burt said. 'We've got enough men to outgun any guards that have been set on the herds. I'll take five with me to run off the bunch to the north. You take the rest and get the Red Diamond stock.'

Carter Ford was undecided. Under normal circumstances, six men was certainly enough to rustle three-hundred head off the range, but a confrontation with a pack of armed men couldn't be discounted and he didn't relish the prospect of being outgunned. The weather, too, seemed like an omen of ill fate; the day had hardly been brightened by sunlight at any point.

Still, he couldn't let Burt's aggression make him look weak. His second-in-command would begin to cast doubts on his own bravery if he didn't emulate his eagerness.

'OK,' he said. 'Let's do it now. The quicker we get the brands burned off them the quicker we can run them to the railhead and get money in our pockets.'

When Clay rode out of Braceville, Frank Sawyer figured that the plot he'd hatched with his uncle and Willard Draysmith was scuppered. The rustlers, he believed, would swiftly reach the conclusion that his involvement with the death of Sour Belly had not been limited to the discovery of the body, that his visit to the stock yard at Tomahawk Wells had been in pursuit of the stolen cattle and that the ranchers were anxious to wreak retribution for the men who had been slaughtered during their last raid. It was probable, therefore, that they would abandon their plans, head for the river and seek safety across the state line. His only advantage was that Carter Ford and his men were unaware that Frank knew the location of their hideout. Ignorant of that fact, the rustlers would consider themselves secure there and have no need for immediate flight. Willard Draysmith had been keen to attack the rustlers in their lair and that now seemed to be the best plan. The sooner it was adopted the greater would be their chance of success.

Accordingly, before quitting Braceville, Frank spoke to the Wheel men who had recently arrived in town and sent them back to their boss with a message to meet up with the Red Diamond crew at the place where the trail climbed from the valley to the outlaws' hideout. In case the rustlers did make a run for the border he urged the Wheel crew to circle round from the river. If they weren't too late then perhaps they would catch them in a pincer movement.

When he got the message, Willard Draysmith lost no time in assembling a dozen riders to accompany him into the Comstock Hills. Armed with rifles and pistols and mounted on stout horses, they left the ranch at a steady gallop. The rain that had been falling most of the day had ceased temporarily but there was no warmth in the air. They rode west, heading for the range where the enticement of cattle had been put to graze. From there they would use a route through the hills that would bring them to the river north of the island crossing, then ride south to the valley in which they would rendezvous with the men from the Red Diamond.

With Beaver Creek behind them, they were fast approaching the grazing herd when one of his men drew Willard's attention to the rising ground a quarter-mile distant. A squad of horsemen had appeared on the brow of a hill and reined to a halt. Willard counted six men and wondered if they were Red Diamond riders, for no other outfit in the area employed so many hands, but his foreman uttered the word that had been lurking in his mind from the first sighting.

'Rustlers.'

When breasting the rise it had been Burt's expectation to see two or three hundred head of cattle spread out on the pasture below. They were prepared for a couple of guards patrolling the herd or camped close by but any resistance they offered would easily be swept away. But a chill ran through Burt's body when he saw the pack of armed men riding hard in his direction.

'Is that a posse?' Johnny wanted to know.

'Worse,' Burt told him. 'We've already been tried by these men and their verdict is guilty. They'll hang us if they catch us.' His last words were yelled so that every man in the group heard him and they followed his example when he turned his horse back towards the hills. They were outgunned; now it was every man for himself.

The crack of gunfire followed them as they rode, the uneven terrain a handicap to the accuracy of their pursuers. No one made an effort to return fire; every man was concentrated on getting the best effort from his mount. They were fleeing for the refuge of the hills, hoping to lose their pursuers among the narrow twists and turns. That goal, however, was difficult to achieve. The gap between themselves and the chasing pack was closing and not even the darkness of the day could obscure the trail that was being kicked up in the soft ground by their galloping horses.

A rifle barked, the sound closer than Burt had expected and an abrupt yell told him that someone had been hit. He glanced behind. The saddle on Will's horse was empty. He shouted in the ear of his own mount and lashed at both flanks with the long reins. It responded as bullets flew close to its rider's head.

To his right he could see Totem draw the long gun from his saddle boot and, unexpectedly, halt his horse. Turning in the saddle with the rifle at his shoulder, he fired two shots at the men behind. Among the band, Totem was renowned for his accuracy with a rifle. Perhaps, Burt thought, the mixed-blood would gain them a few moments to open up a gap. The hope was in vain. Johnny, riding by, his face drawn and white spoke with a tremulous voice.

'They've got Totem. What do we do, Burt?'

'Keep riding,' he answered, pointing to a valley opening that the other three riders were hoping was their route to safety. 'Follow them,' he told Johnny and allowed him to ride ahead.

Lead was flying all around and Burt knew that if he didn't get out of range soon then he too would be lying dead in the mud. Above the sound of gunshots and drumming hoof beats he heard another cry of pain. Up ahead, the reins still gripped in his right hand, someone threw their arms skywards, yanking up the horse's head, causing it to rear suddenly then topple backwards onto the ground. A following horse collided with it and was brought down. The other two riders were forced to check their mounts to avert the catastrophe but the loss of momentum was fatal to their chances of survival. Although there were no shouts of triumph, Burt could sense the cowboys speeding in to finish off the fight.

After sending Johnny in pursuit of the other gang members, Burt had veered to the left and followed a line that put some bushes between him and his pursuers. They weren't dense enough to obscure him from the view of anyone who was watching him closely, but, for the moment, the mayhem caused by the fallen horse had drawn everyone's attention away from him. Taking advantage of the situation, Burt raced his pony down a dip that led into a narrow gully in which he hoped to escape the fury of those seeking retribution for dead men and stolen beef. Suddenly, behind him, he heard a fusillade of gunfire, the sounds suppressed by the hills so that they carried to him as little more than crackles, but he knew their deadly significance. The rest of the crew were dead. The cattlemen had their revenge and had taken it swiftly. They hadn't even delayed long enough to stretch anyone's neck.

Burt kept his horse running a while but it was tiring quickly now. It was wheezing as it struggled forward. Easing it to a halt, Burt considered what to do next. He could either make his way back to the hideout and link up with Carter Ford and the men who had gone to raid the Red Diamond range, or head for the river and seek safety across the border. He favoured the latter; there was no guarantee that Carter had fared any better rustling Red Diamond stock, but his horse needed to rest awhile. He couldn't tackle the powerful river on such a weary animal.

He rested for half an hour in the lee of big oak but when the rain began to fall he decided he couldn't delay the crossing any longer. His horse was breathing easier when he checked its girth strap and raised a foot to the stirrup. A voice, weary and full of sadness for what was about to happen, spoke behind him.

'Throw the gun away before you climb up there,' said Willard Draysmith.

Burt turned his head to see the three men who sat their horses a dozen yards away. He could see the tracks on the ground that had led them to this place. A noose had been thrown over the branch of a nearby tree.

'You're not going to hang me,' Burt said.

'Then we'll shoot you,' Willard told him and three guns were cocked in readiness. 'You've killed and you've stolen from me. It's time to pay the price.'

Burt knew there was no way out but he wasn't going to go without a fight. His hand reached for his pistol but instantly, three bullets smashed into his chest. They left him there face down in the mud.

Titus Sawyer had spoken to the men gathered in the yard and told them he wouldn't hold it against anyone who chose not to be with him when he attacked the outlaws' hideout. There were no dissenters. Not only had every man known the men who had been killed but, because of the bandits' ruthlessness, they knew that they, too, could fall victim of any future raid. They all saddled up ready to ride.

Linc Bywater was especially keen to join the group. He'd pestered Frank all the way back from town in the buckboard, insisting that Doctor Jones had declared him fit to ride again. Frank hadn't believed him and knew that hard riding was beyond his current ability but said he would allow it if he could saddle his own horse. When everyone else was galloping out of the yard, Linc had nothing more than the blanket over his animal's back. He'd asked for help but none had been forthcoming. As much as they sympathised with his desire to be involved in the capture of the men who had left him for dead, they knew that in the event of a gun battle it would be every man for himself. It was clear to everyone that Linc's recovery was not yet complete. He'd cursed as they rode away; cursed them for leaving him behind and cursed the wound that had weakened his body.

The Red Diamond operated on a smaller workforce than the Wheel. Consequently the band that left the ranch was smaller than the dozen assembled by Willard Draysmith. Six men, including his nephew Frank and Mustang Moore rode with Titus Sawyer, but when they reached Beaver Creek they were bolstered by another two. Zig Braun and 'Skinny' Clark, who had been posted to keep watch on the decoy herd, pulled up their horses on the other bank.

Zig pointed across the range behind. 'They've taken the cattle,' he yelled and, as though he needed to justify his desertion of the stock, added, 'We didn't try to stop them. Like you ordered, we were heading for the ranch to let you know.'

Frank was pleased they'd caught the rustlers redhanded. His uncle, he knew, was already convinced of their guilt and intent upon killing them wherever he met them, but Frank was more comfortable with the undeniable proof of discovery in the act. Titus nodded an approval of Zig and Skinny's action. 'How far ahead are they?'

'Two miles. We'll catch them before they reach the high ground.'

Rain spattered on the face of Titus Sawyer when he asked how many rustlers had taken the herd.

'Can't give an exact number,' Zig told him, 'but I reckon we're even matched.' Skinny Clark agreed.

'OK,' said Titus, 'let's get our cattle back.'

Rain was now falling heavily, sweeping like a curtain across the open pasture as the wind gusted over the hills ahead. The rustlers needed to be attentive to the cattle that were reluctant to be driven headlong into it, which contributed to the ability of the Red Diamond riders to overtake them almost unobserved. In fact, Carter Ford had dismissed any thought of pursuit after finding and chasing away the two men who had been close to the herd. He was unaware that they were obeying orders when they quit the herd and were not fleeing for their lives.

The drag riders were the first to come under fire, bullets striking them without warning. One fell to the ground like a heavy sack of vegetables. He bounced once then lay still. The other drag man who had twisted to look behind at the sound of the first gunshot fell with one foot caught in a stirrup.

His horse bolted and his body bounced and bumped violently as it raced alongside the slow-moving herd.

The Red Diamond riders had split into two groups, one led by Titus Sawyer and the other by his nephew. They rode down the flanks of the herd ready to combat any resistance from the rustlers. It was one of the outlaw outriders who, seeing the body of a fellow gang member being dragged by the runaway horse, became aware of the attack. Drawing his gun he fired two shots at the fast approaching avengers.

Those shots were answered by the guns of the men under Frank's command. That rustler fell dead and the cracks of gunfire had another effect that aided the attackers. The cattle, which until this moment had been reluctant to move, now reacted in their typical, inbred, nervous manner. They began to run so suddenly and swiftly that the rustlers who had been guiding the way at the head of the herd now found themselves surrounded by cattle. The barging and bellowing critters buffeted, squashed and prodded those men's horses into panicked flight. Carter Ford allowed his mount its head and it raced clear of the stampeding herd. The other, however, became embroiled in the tumult as, unrestricted, the front cattle tried to veer away from the rain that was lashing their faces while the rear animals, fleeing the sounds of gunfire, rushed hard upon them. In the chaos, the rustler's horse went down and he was trampled to death beneath the thundering hoofs.

Five rustlers were being chased by Titus Sawyer, Zig Braun, Skinny and two other Red Diamond riders. They chased them for a mile, with shots exchanged and casualties sustained by both parties, but the outcome was never in doubt. Zig Braun took a nick on his hip, which was painful but not lethal. One of the outlaws took a similar slight hit to a shoulder but it proved to be a death sentence for him. When he fell from his horse he was pounced upon by two Red Diamond men and strung up alongside the only other survivor of the chase.

'All accounted for,' Titus said with a dreadful tone of satisfaction.

But his nephew didn't agree. At one point in the running battle he'd glimpsed a figure in a long fringed coat but in the aftermath he hadn't been counted among the dead. Carter Ford was still abroad, making a run for the hills.

ELEVEN

When he'd cut away from the stampede, Carter Ford had found himself close to a knoll atop of which grew an old forked cottonwood. As cattle bellowed and ran wild-eyed across the soft, churning pasture and men strove to kill each other he managed to escape the observation of everyone and climb that knoll. Using the tree for cover he watched the ensuing conflict, saw his men fall under the guns of Titus Sawyer and his crew and knew he was lucky to be alive. As the cowboys prepared to lynch the last of his men he turned away, hoping the oncoming night and persistent rain would deter a prolonged search for survivors. He went down the back side of the knoll that hid him from sight as he crossed the meadow towards the nearest fold between the low Comstocks. Anxious though he was to put distance between himself and the hanging tree, he didn't ask a great pace from his mount. He moved as gently and quietly as possible in the hope that he wouldn't alert the cattlemen. He would make his way to the hideout in the hills and meet up with Burt's crew who would have the cattle they'd run off the Wheel range.

Lynching was a distasteful business for Frank. He knew it was the law of the west, that rustlers knew the penalty if they got caught with another man's livestock, but he'd spent a lot of time working hand-in-glove with city lawmen, and their respect for trials and judges had rubbed off on him. So he'd gone back along the trail of the stampede hoping to find some sign of the missing leader of the rustler gang. His eyes picked out a trail kicked up by a single horse. It was heading towards a tree-topped knoll, but before he could follow it a lone rider came into view from the direction of Beaver Creek.

When the rider got within hailing distance, Frank called to him. 'Who saddled that horse?'

'I did,' lied Linc Bywater. In fact the cook, who had been ordered to stay behind, had harnessed the animal for him. 'You said I could ride with you,' he added defiantly. The effort it had taken for him to ride so far from the Red Diamond showed clearly on his face.

'It's all over,' Frank told him.

They looked in the direction of the group that were three hundred yards distant and could see the bodies swinging from the branch of a tree.

'What are you doing?' Linc wanted to know.

'Guess I'm making sure we've got everyone.'

He rode to the top of the knoll, paused and examined the line of hoof prints leading towards the hills, then kicked off in pursuit. Even the limited tracking abilities he possessed were enough to tell him that the man ahead was not moving quickly. The hoof prints were deep; the animal's weight was settling on the ground longer than if it had been at full gallop. Consequently, he didn't spare his own horse, eager to catch up to the killer as quickly as possible. Although he assumed that Carter Ford was heading for the cabins in the hill he couldn't be certain. Perhaps he meant to make a run for the river in the hope that crossing the border would save him from pursuit. Visibility was diminishing; he needed to wipe the rainwater from his eyes.

He had followed the tracks into the fold between the hills, a narrow route that seemed familiar to him. He guessed it was the trail that he and Mustang had used that first morning together. Memory told him that there were no natural turnoffs along this trail. If Carter Ford was heading for the hideout then either he had to cut his own trail over the hills or he had to go through to the river and ride north until he reached the valley that would give him access to the track that led to the hideout in the hills. It was at that moment that the first flash of lightning split the heavily clouded sky, providing a vivid glimpse of what lay ahead. At a bend in the corridor, at walking pace, a horseman could be seen. He was bent forward across his horse's neck as

152

though using his head to butt his way through the storm. His hat was suffering the full force of the assailing squall, his face turned aside so that he was looking back along the trail he had just ridden. In that brief moment of light they saw each other.

Frank Sawyer loosened the buttons on his heavy, sodden jacket, but by the time he'd pulled his pistol from the holster on his right hip Carter Ford had disappeared from sight. With hands and feet he asked his horse for more effort, spurred it on towards the bend in the trail around which his quarry had disappeared. When he reached it, Ford wasn't in sight, but the muddy tracks stretched out ahead. The valley had developed a slight slope, one that would eventually bring him down to the riverside. He kicked on, determined that Carter would not escape punishment.

As expected, when he emerged from that narrow trail through the hills, Ford's tracks turned to the north. At this point he was on an embankment that, here and there, bulged over the river that was roaring and racing more than twenty feet below. The sodden ground had become quagmire soft and Frank's horse was struggling to lift its feet from the clinging mud. For a moment it almost came to a standstill. Frank yelled encouragement in its ear, knowing the beast wasn't objecting to the chase but simply floundering in conditions that would be almost impossible to overcome if he had to tackle them afoot.

Suddenly a shot rang out. A lance of flame that cut momentarily through the gloom was accompanied by a jarring impact high on his left shoulder. He was tumbled out of his saddle with such awkwardness that the gun was dislodged from his hand and his horse was brought to its knees. He could hear it crying in distress as he began to slide down the muddy embankment. The pain in his shoulder was less severe than he'd expected from a gunshot wound, similar, in fact, to a strong punch to the shoulder, but even so it restricted the use of his left arm as he tried to put a brake on his descent. Every effort to halt his downward slide succeeded only in filling his hands with mud.

The sound of another gunshot reached him, muffled by the mud that filled his ears. No further damage was inflicted; Frank wasn't even aware if it had come close to hitting him. For the moment, his every thought, every instinct was dominated by his uncontrollable descent through the cloying mud. If he failed to arrest it he would be carried to a watery death in the raging river. Such a fate didn't appeal but his frantic struggles were having the reverse effect to what he intended; his plunge to the bottom was gathering momentum.

Then he struck a tree and stopped almost abruptly. The force of the impact was cushioned by the mud and his heavy jacket, otherwise the breath would have been forced out of his body. As it was, his mind was still clear enough to reach out with his

154

right hand and grasp a willowy offshoot at the base of the trunk. Slippery though his hand was, he knew he had to hang onto it if he was to have any chance of survival.

Once again a gunshot cracked. It sounded closer than the others and a lump of bark jumped off the tree behind which Frank sheltered. He raised his head to seek out the location of his enemy. Another shot forced him to lower it again but he'd had time enough to understand the predicament he was in.

In defiance of the weather and conditions, his long fringed coat flapping in the rain-carrying wind, Carter Ford was advancing towards him, rifle in hand, eager to finish off his adversary and get a clear run to safety. He placed his feet carefully, ensuring that he didn't slip so that he, too, wasn't sent hurtling down the embankment in an uncontrollable skid. The lack of return fire was assurance enough that his hunter was unarmed and at his mercy. To verify that fact he fired his rifle twice more, each bullet gouging huge chunks out of the tree trunk that was the only barrier between the foes.

Frank waited, barely moving, almost holding his breath. There was mud in his mouth, up his nose and around his eyes but he ignored the irritation they caused. He could do nothing but await his executioner. The next bullet would end his life.

A strange noise reached Frank. It wasn't loud but the roar of the river diminished every other sound.

It was Carter Ford's yell that prompted Frank to raise his head above the roots of the tree. The noise came from above. It was an ominous, wet, plopping sound that continued until one of the high overhangs broke away from the embankment. A wave of mud slid down the slope, ploughing an unstoppable course to the river below. Carter Ford raised his arms as though commanding it to halt but he had no control over it. One moment he was there and the next he was gone, wiped from the earth as had been the fate of that whole Mandan village years earlier.

A spluttering cough broke from Frank's mouth. Not only did it help to clear out the mud but it also marked the relief he was experiencing. He'd survived the gun of his foe but his jubilation was only momentary. More mud was beginning to slip from the top of the embankment, this time on a course that was likely to claim him as the next victim. The tree seemed to be his only source of refuge. If he could climb onto one of the lower branches he had a chance of staying clear of the mudslide. Its approach, however, was too quick. It was almost upon him before his body could react to the messages from his brain. It seemed inevitable that he would be swept to his doom.

The voice that called his name might have been dismissed as a delusion of hope if a rope hadn't snaked through the air to reach him a mere second before his feet were taken from under him. He clung to the rope with his right hand, somehow managed to twist it around the wrist as the vile flow tried to carry him down to the river. He was face down and covered in mud, unable to find the necessary purchase that would enable his feet to push against the slimy tide. Only desperation kept him fighting, lifting his head from the morass in an instinctive search for air, while fearing that his right arm might be pulled out of its socket as the rope by which it was secured provided resistance against the downward pull of the sludge.

Although the ordeal seemed interminable, it did in fact last only a few seconds. The knowledge that he had survived another threat to his life occurred when he eventually realized that most of the movement was not caused by the sweeping hillside mud but by his body being dragged uphill. When it came to a stop, Linc Bywater sank down at his side. The young man removed the rope from Frank's wrist, the other end of which was tied to his saddle-horn. Exhausted, barely alive, one with a black face and the other deathly white, they knelt side by side in the torrential rain.

Three days later, with the long overdue sun searing Braceville's main street, Frank entered the town's new eating place. He'd failed in his promise to be the first customer; it had taken him a couple of days to recover from the battering he'd received on the banks of the big river, but he had no intention of leaving town without first visiting Meg Rouse and Alice. The interior wasn't spacious and most of the dozen covered tables were occupied, but a place was found for Frank and Mustang, who accompanied him. In fact, Mustang had described the internal fixtures and fittings in such fine detail that nothing in the place was a surprise to Frank. Indeed, he had begun to wonder what future role Mustang intended to fulfil in this place. The greeting the older man received from Meg Rouse more or less convinced Frank that Mustang's days at the Red Diamond were numbered and that, it seemed, was a sentiment to which Alice, too, adhered. He'd watched her taking orders, carrying trays, pouring coffee and chatting with customers with verve and a smile, but when he spoke to her alone she confessed that the life of a waitress was not for her.

'I want to dance,' she told him. 'Meg is happy to have a settled home but I miss the open road. When things are settled between them,' she'd indicated Meg and Mustang, 'I intend to head east. There are big theatres in New York. I know I'm good enough to get a job there.'

She joined him on the boardwalk when he climbed on his horse and said goodbye.

'When do you leave?' she asked.

'I head for the train station in Silver City in the morning. I'll be back in San Francisco by the end of the week.'

Alice smiled. 'Perhaps we'll meet again,' she said.

'I understand they have big theatres in San Francisco, too.'

Frank tipped his hat and rode across the street.

It had been his intention to go into the Diamond Queen but Lulu was leaning against a boardwalk post smoking a black cigarillo, so he remained in the saddle.

'I'm leaving town,' he said. 'Just wanted to say thank you.'

'You've already done that,' she said. 'It doesn't need repeating.'

'No,' he said, 'last time I said thank you for what you did for the kid. This time it's for what you've done for me.'

'I haven't done anything,' she told him.

'You saved my life,' he said.

She blew smoke into the air. 'How do you figure that?'

'We caught up with the rustlers.'

'I've heard the story,' she said, 'it's been told and retold in there,' she inclined her head towards the Diamond Queen's doors. 'Red Diamond and Wheel riders out-bragging each other.'

'Guess that's the way it is with the victors.'

'Doesn't explain why you think I saved your life.'

'Because young Linc couldn't have arrived in the nick of time to save me if you hadn't brought him back from death's door.'

She made a noise that scoffed at the suggestion.

'Think about it,' he said, 'good deeds spread to

159

more good deeds.'

'You're not trying to convert me to a pure life, are you, Mr Sawyer?'

'Perhaps, but more importantly I want you to know that you can count on my help if you ever need it.'

She smiled and inclined her head in acknowledgement. Frank wasn't sure if the gesture was gracious or mocking but he touched his hat as though about to depart. Even though he knew they were nothing but ships that pass in the night, he was intrigued by her, perhaps even hopeful that they would meet again.

'I suppose you should tell me your proper name,' he said, 'in case you ever want to contact me.'

For a moment she delayed any answer then stepped down onto the street and beckoned him to lower his head as though what she had to impart was a secret.

'Lulu,' she whispered. 'My name is Lulu.'

When she returned to the boardwalk she stood with one hand resting on a cocked hip, the gaze in her large, dark eyes forbidding any criticism of the life she'd chosen. Eventually she smiled, a slight thing, as though she'd recognized the hope he harboured of another encounter. 'Come and see me next time you visit your uncle,' she told him. 'I'll be here.'